WHAT THE PARROT TOLD ALICE

WHAT THE PARROT TOLD ALICE

BY DALE SMITH

ILLUSTRATED BY JOHN BARDWELL

Published by
DEER CREEK PUBLISHING
P.O. Box 2402
Nevada City, CA 95959

ISBN 0-9651452-7-1
Library of Congress Catalog Card Number: 96-96118

Smith, Dale, 1945

What the parrot told Alice / by Dale Smith ; illustrated by John Bardwell.

p.cm

SUMMARY: Alice's friend Bo Parrot tells her about the smuggling trade in rare birds, and its consequences.

1. Environmentalism—Juvenile fiction. 2. Parrots—Juvenile fiction. 3. Wild bird trade—Juvenile fiction. 4. Wild animal trade—Juvenile fiction. 5. Smuggling—Juvenile fiction. I.
Title.

PS3569.M4584W43 1996 813'.54
QBI96-20241

Book design by Dale Smith
Manufactured in the United States of America

10 9 8 7 6 5 4 3 2 1

CONTENTS

This book is dedicated to my daughter Alice,
and to all the children who will inherit the earth.

And to my mother, and the memory of my father,
who listened only with his heart.

In the end we will conserve only what we love.
We will love only what we understand.
We will understand only what we have been taught.

Baba Dioum

ACKNOWLEDGEMENTS

I would like to thank the following people for their input, insights and contributions to the writing of *What the Parrot Told Alice*:

Destiny Baker, Grace Barbor, John Bardwell, Christine Butterfield, Marjorie Doggett, Cheryl and Blake Dorse, Lauri Jon Elliot, Thaisa Frank, David Fritz, Kathy Gillivan, Laurel Hilde, Kelly Houston, Larry and Lisa Keenan, Rick Klein, Caroline LaPrade, Tom Lippert, Rosemary Low, John Perrine, Dr. Shirley McGreal, Paul McHugh, Dr. Irene M. Pepperberg, Kris Sarri, and my sister, Sherri Fritz Smith.

I am especially indebted to my lifelong friends Suzanna Camejo and Jack Izzo, S.J., for their many valuable suggestions. To Fred Bauer, who introduced me to the world of parrots, I extend my gratitude. And, I would like to thank Pam Eaton for her immeasurable moral support.

FOREWORD

"Starting in 1799, Baron Alexander von Humboldt, the intrepid German explorer who helped convince his friend Simon Bolivar that Latin America should fight for independence, spent five years in the jungles of the Western Hemisphere, where he claimed to have found a very old parrot that had been raised as a pet by the Ature Indians, a tribe that had become extinct. The parrot, Humboldt wrote, marveling, was the last being on earth to use their language."

From the article "Parrots"
by Jane and Michael Stern
published in the July 30, 1990
New Yorker. Used by permission.

CHAPTER 1

IT WAS THIRTY YEARS AGO TODAY

Bougainville, The Solomon Islands, 1966

As Manao walked from his family's leaf hut at the edge of the jungle to the magician's house at the center of the village, he noticed a cluster of fireflies hovering against the dark forest wall. He looked away quickly, pretending not to notice. To see a cluster of fireflies was bad luck—fireflies meant a bush demon lurked nearby. Though he had never seen a bush demon, or even knew what one looked like, Manao didn't want to find out now. His long legs broke into a trot, and the moist earth was left with impressions of his bare feet. His naked shoulders soon glistened. His necklace of shell beads stuck to his skin and rivulets of sweat coursed through his dense, tightly curled hair and down his brow.

The drums beat louder as he approached the center of the village, echoing the beat of his heart. Fires flickered in the stone pits outside the leaf huts he passed and he called out greetings to his friends as he ran by, but none of them returned his greeting. He knew why, and he didn't blame them. He'd made a mistake, and that mistake was why he'd been summoned on this sticky evening to the magician's house.

Like all houses in the village, the magician's was built on pilings, above the ebb and flow of flood waters. Manao climbed the steps and wiped his brow. He wiped his hands on his lap-lap and scratched timidly at the palm thatch wall of the magician's house.

"Come in, Manao," called Yehamu the magician. "I've been expecting you."

Manao drew a deep breath and entered the hut. Yehamu was seated on the floor made of split palm logs. The light from an oil lamp illuminated the long bone that passed through Yehamu's nose and the chalky white lines drawn on his dark forehead and cheeks. It also shone on the stained New York Yankees T-shirt that clung to his body. Yehamu was an old man, the oldest among the Siwai tribe. In the shadows, on a platform against the wall, Manao's mother sat wrapped in a cloak of sorrow.

"Sit," said Yehamu, solemnly gesturing to a mat before him. His tone was neither friendly nor unfriendly, and Manao obeyed.

"You know why you are here?" asked Yehamu.

"Yes," said Manao.

"Tell me," said the magician, "so we both understand."

"I cut down the biggest tree in our forest," said Manao, his eyes cast down. He looked across the dancing flame at the baseball image on Yehamu's shirt and wondered what it meant.

"And why did you do this?" asked Yehamu.

"Because I wanted to make the biggest log drum the village had ever known and present it as a gift to our community," said Manao.

"But you knew it was wrong to take the biggest and oldest tree in our forest, did you not?" said Yehamu.

"Yes," said Manao, meekly.

"Then what is your excuse?" said Yehamu.

"I told you," said Manao. "I wanted to make a gift to our village."

"That is your *reason*," said the magician, "but what is your *excuse?*"

"My excuse?" said Manao, shaking his head. "I guess I don't have one."

"I agree," said Yehamu. "You may have a reason, but you are without an excuse."

Manao and Yehamu sat in silence while the magician's words settled over the boy. Then Yehamu said, "This is the twelfth year of your life, Manao. By now you should know the balance that exists between our people and the forest which gives us life. This knowledge should be a part of you. You should know better than to take the biggest, or oldest, or most fertile, or most beautiful of the bounty which surrounds us, should you not, Manao?"

"Yes," said Manao. "I should."

"Yet you have demonstrated by your actions that you do not," said Yehamu.

In the shadows, Manao's mother began to weep. Her tears ran down her creased cheeks like rain spilling down a leaf in the forest.

"There is an important lesson you must learn, Manao," said Yehamu, gravely. "I must teach you what you have failed to learn from your elders, and what you have been unable to observe on your own."

"What will you do to me?" asked Manao, wide-eyed, staring at his own reflection in the magician's eyes.

"Your spirit will inhabit the body of a forest dweller," said the magician.

"A forest dweller?" said Manao.

"A bird, Manao," said Yehamu. "A parrot."

"A parrot?" said Manao.

"You will become a parrot and you will learn to see the world through the eyes of a parrot," said the magician.

"No," moaned Manao's mother, unable to keep silent any longer. "He is my child! I suckled him! Do not change him just because you can!"

"You will have the gift of language," Yehamu continued, ignoring the pleas of the woman. "Just as the parrot speaks in many tongues, so shall you. You will be able to speak from the silence of your mind, and your words will be illuminated by the illusion of your presence, but this gift will have its limitations."

"Limitations?" said Manao.

"You will be able to exchange thoughts with a human being, but only *one* human being, so your choice must be a wise one," said the magician. "The human you choose must be sensitive to your message and understand the importance of sharing it with others."

"My message?" asked Manao.

"The message of balance and harmony that must exist between humans and the wild world," said Yehamu. "Do you understand what you must do, Manao?"

Manao drew a deep breath. "I think so," he said. "But how will I know the right person to choose?"

"That will become clear to you," said Yehamu. "But you might consider a child."

"A child?" said Manao.

"Everyone has a future, but the future extends deeper into time for a child than it does for a man my age, or a woman like your mother. A child will have more opportunities to pass the message along to future generations."

Manao felt suddenly overwhelmed by his burden. "But will I ever be free again? Will I ever be Manao, like I am now?"

"You will be a parrot, Manao. The experiences of a parrot and the knowledge gained through those experiences will be yours to share. When you have passed the gift of awareness to a human being who will make a difference in the world—only then will you be free."

"Free to be Manao again?"

"Free to be free," said the magician.

"But will I be *me* again?" said Manao.

The magician looked at Manao and lit his pipe and drew the smoke deep into his lungs. "That's up to you. You will become whoever you are," said the magician, and Manao thought he saw the old man wink.

A spark from the wick of the oil lamp spiraled toward the thatched roof. As his eyes followed the spark, the light in Manao's eyes left him and joined the spark in a bright union. A draft carried the light through the door and into the night where it landed on the wings of a moth resting on the thatched roof. The moth began to glow like an ember then flew into the forest where it was swallowed by darkness. And everywhere was the insistent beating of drums.

At that exact moment, in a nest in the hollow of a dead tree in the forest, a fine web of lines appeared on the surface of an egg and a featherless, blind parrot pushed its way into the world.

BARDWELL

CHAPTER 2

YOUR VOICE IN MY HEAD

The Lost Coast, California, 1996

The wind whispered beneath the raven's wings like a secret. As far as his sharp eyes could see stood stands of trees and the rolling unfenced meadows of California's Lost Coast. As an updraft carried him higher, he watched his own shadow rise and fall over the landscape.

Far below, a herd of deer grazing in a dew-sparkling field cast long shadows in the morning light. The raven's shadow passed over mallards and canvasbacks at rest on a muddy half-full pond, its surface smooth and dull as an unwashed window. Chocolate-colored curls of mud at the edge of the pond were reminders of a long rainless summer. Beneath the trees and across open flats, dirt roads crisscrossed the hills, ending at an old farm, or ranch, or a modern homestead with solar panels glinting in the sun. The raven banked left and just for a moment followed a pickup truck speeding along the road below. Its tires kicked up dusty clouds that settled on the tangled blackberry bushes.

This morning, the raven's goal was a familiar walnut tree at the edge of a meadow. Most of the leaves on the tree were still green and glossy, but a recent cold spell had turned the leaves along one branch a crisp yellow, and they turned and twisted in the faint breeze like a school of tropical fish riding a current.

By late summer the walnut pods hung cracked and available all over the tree. The wrinkled, brain-textured nutmeats inside made sweet food for a raven with patience and skill. Dropping down and swooping between the tall fir trees, the raven extended his claws and landed on the branch with the yellowing leaves. His silky black wings wrapped his shadowless body like a perfectly tailored cape as he rode the bobbing limb. He announced his arrival with a rough, throaty call that echoed through the surrounding dark forest.

Hungrily, the raven ripped a walnut pod from its stem, then glided effortlessly to a spot in the meadow. He dropped the pod on the dry grass and, using his beak, dug a shallow cavity in the soft earth to steady the pod. Cocking his head, he studied the pod to make certain it would not roll on the slight downward slope. He raised his head and began to strike the pod with the chisel of his closed beak with the steady rhythm of a metronome. Chips of tough green husk flew into the air as he drove the pod into the soft soil.

Nestled into the hillside near the walnut tree stood a house with large picture windows and views of the meadow and surrounding forest. At the meadow's far edge, where the land flattened out, lay a garden and orchard. The curling leaves on the plum, peach, pear and apple trees were every shade and mottled pattern of yellow, red, orange and purple. A rickety eight-foot fence surrounded the orchard and garden to keep out the deer. Beyond the garden was the edge of the forest, a diverse tangle of madrone, fir, tan oak, and an occasional bay laurel, which the locals called pepperwood. The coast mountains, rising and falling like earthen waves all the way to the sea, were visible between the spires of fir. As they receded from the house, the ridges became lighter and lighter and the last ridge, on this particular morning, was a pale wash of periwinkle blue.

The raven didn't know it, but he was watched from within the house by a small green parrot and a twelve-year-old girl, whose name was Alice.

What must he weigh? the parrot wondered as he shuffled back and forth along his perch on top of his living room cage. A *couple of pounds at least...certainly more than a chicken. And his wing span's got to be three feet, maybe more. He's so shiny, so black, so alluring in his stark simplicity. And his tail, what happened to his tail? He's missing a feather or two from the center of his tail. How did that happen?* wondered the parrot. A *fox? A mountain lion? A bad landing?*

Of all the birds that lived in the hills—the thrushes, jays, owls, hawks and kites, the quail, the woodpeckers and flickers, the chickadees, juncos, wrens and nuthatches—the raven was the most talented. He was intelligent in a way that only birds can express. And there was no denying his cleverness. You wouldn't see a thrush or a flicker bury a walnut, the parrot mused. The raven seemed to know there was a future, and it needed to be prepared for. There was no doubt in the parrot's mind that the raven was the indisputable king of the local sky.

When the raven's beak broke through the rock hard shell, he cocked his head and let out a triumphant caw-caw-caw which drowned out the melodic trills and whistles of the songbirds and caused the parrot to wince. As much as he admired the raven, the parrot was jealous of him, too.

The raven's confident call and swift, precise flight reminded the parrot of who he was, and was not.

You're just a bat with feathers, thought the parrot with jealous disgust. *Nothing but an overgrown, tarred and feathered chicken.*

Alice, an only child, was a tall girl with flaxen hair, olive brown eyes, and a splatter of freckles across her nose. During the school year she lived with her father on forty acres of wilderness. Most mornings she watched the raven's antics while she waited for her ride to school. This morning she pressed her forehead against the sliding glass door and thought, "That raven's such an amazing bird."

The parrot looked up from his feed cup and cocked his densely feathered green head. *What was that?* he thought. He had heard something, a sucking sound, like a tire rolling through soft mud. *Weird*, he mused, eyeing Alice suspiciously over the curve of his beak and going a little cross-eyed in the process. *That's the strangest thing I've ever heard.*

"I wonder why he's burying all those walnuts?" thought Alice.

The parrot squawked loudly and nearly tumbled from his perch. This time the words that formed Alice's thought had appeared in his mind's eye like chalk marks on a blackboard. It gave him the willies. *Those couldn't be Alice's thoughts, could they?* he wondered. *Parrots don't hear humans' thoughts.* A bit unnerved, he returned to his breakfast.

"Maybe my dad knows why he's doing that," thought Alice.

The parrot's head popped out of his feed cup like a tightly sprung jack-in-the-box. This time there was no mistaking it. Alice's thought had floated through his mind as clear and clean as a flute solo.

The parrot cocked his head and drew a calming breath. He concentrated on Alice and thought, "The raven buries walnuts to soften the shells."

"Oh, *now* I get it," Alice responded, without uttering a sound. "The raven really is as smart as he seems."

The parrot looked around the room, but there was no one near but Alice. He drew a breath and rustled his tail feathers. "Are you talking to *me?*" he said, in a perfect imitation of Robert DeNiro.

Alice, who often carried on imaginary conversations with the deer and foxes and raccoons that wandered into the meadow, looked in the parrot's direction and said, "Yes...I...I guess I am."

"This is too strange," thought the parrot, pacing the length of his perch. He eyed his reflection each time he passed the mirror above his feed cup just to make sure he was still there, still in the present. Then a memory flickered through his mind like a flashing lighthouse beacon and he remembered the words of the magician from so many years ago: *"You will be able to exchange thoughts with a human being, but only one human being, so your choice must be a wise one."*

"Could this be the moment I've waited for all these years?" thought the parrot. *"Is this the human Yehamu told me to watch for, the one who will make a difference, the one who will set me free?"*

The parrot crouched low on his perch, and leaned toward Alice. With his mind fully focused and his beak tightly closed, he said, "Can you really *hear* me, Alice?"

"I can't really *hear* you, but I can hear your voice in my head," said Alice tentatively, rubbing her temples. "It's kinda *weird*...like an echo or something."

"That's how it is for me, too, but you sound like you're at the bottom of a well," said the parrot. "It's strange because you're not really...you know, talking."

"I know. I'm just *thinking*," said Alice.

"This is it," thought the parrot, suddenly aware that time had not yet moved through the moment as it should have. *"Alice is the human I've waited for all these years...Alice!"*

"I wonder why I haven't heard you think before?" said the parrot, trying to control his excitement.

"I don't know," said Alice, shrugging her shoulders. "Maybe you weren't ready."

"Maybe *I* wasn't ready?" said the parrot. "Well, I don't know about that. *I've* been ready for a long time...at least I thought I was. Maybe you're the one who wasn't ready."

"What do you mean you've been ready for a long time?" asked Alice.

For a moment the parrot considered whether to reveal his true self to Alice, but he decided it was better to show Alice than to tell her. *"Besides,"* he thought, *"I'm not sure if I know who my true self is anymore."*

"And what do you mean *I* wasn't ready?" Alice added, somewhat indignantly.

"Well, maybe I didn't *know* you were ready, how's that? Maybe we both just sort of, you know, woke up," said the parrot. Then he began to sing, slightly off key, a song Alice's Dad used to play over and over again, so many times, in fact, that the parrot thought he would lose his mind. "Something's happening here..."

"...what it is ain't exactly clear," Alice chimed in.

A moment of silence settled between them like a feather floating to the bottom of a cage. Alice sat on the stairs that led down to the living room from the kitchen and put her elbows on her knees. Her eyebrows arched over her eyes like a pair of question marks. "There's something I've always been curious about," she wondered, in her silent way. "Is Bo Parrot your *real* name? I mean, it seems like such an odd name for a parrot."

The parrot shuffled to the edge of his perch. "Odd? You think my name is *odd?*" said Bo Parrot, the pupils of his orange soda eyes pulsing with excitement.

"Well, maybe just a little," said Alice.

"My parents named me Avu, after a river in the Solomon Islands."

"The Solomon Islands? Is that where you come from?" said Alice. "I don't remember studying them in my geography class. Where are they?"

"About as far away from here as you can get, down in the South Pacific near New Guinea," said the parrot. "Eclectus parrots—that's my species, Eclectus—are native to the Solomons."

"The Solomon Islands," said Alice, dreamily. "They sound so exotic."

"Exotic? Well, it's a lot different than here, that's for sure."

"What's it like?"

"C'mon, I'll take you," said the parrot. "Close your eyes and imagine a beach with sand as black and fine as powdered charcoal and as endless as a freeway. Imagine cocoa palms swaying along the shore, can you hear them rustling in the breeze, Alice?"

"Yes, and I can see them, too," said Alice, her eyes tightly closed, her lips smiling wide over her braces.

"That's good," said the parrot, "that's very good. Now picture mango trees along a river, see how their roots grow right out of the water? And can you see those mountain peaks poking through the clouds? Ah, it's paradise all right, that's for sure."

"It sure is beautiful," said Alice.

"Now imagine a sky as blue as the sea, and a sea as blue as the sky. And a jungle that's as lush and green as, well...as green as me, actually."

"It all seems so perfect," said Alice, her eyes still closed. Then her eyes popped open and the picture of paradise she held in her mind disappeared like a postcard dropped into a mailbox. "But, if your parents named you Avu," she said suddenly, "why are you called Bo Parrot?"

"I've been called Bo Parrot since your father found me in a Texas pet store, a long, long time ago—way before you were born. I mean, he didn't know my name was Avu, so he gave me a new one. Bo's sort of a nickname—short for Rainbow."

"*Rainbow?*" said Alice, wrinkling her freckled nose. "Did he name you that because your feathers are so colorful?"

"I'm proud of my plumage," said Bo Parrot, showing off the splash of red hidden beneath his wings. His flight feathers were iridescent green on top and indigo blue beneath, the color of the sea far from shore. At the bend of his wings was a narrow piping of electric neon blue. His tail feathers, which were quite stubby, were blue-green on one side and nickel gray on the other and there was a faint, ragged band of dirty yellow at their tips. His beak was the color of a Halloween pumpkin and as smooth as a polished precious stone. At first glance, his beak seemed too large for his head, like it belonged on some other, larger parrot. But his eyes were small, like orange pinheads buried in a green velvet cushion. The fine green feathers that covered his head and neck were dense, more like fur than feathers. For a parrot only slightly larger than a pigeon, Bo Parrot presented an intricate and complicated image to the world.

"You look like you belong on MTV," said Alice just as a horn honked outside.

At that moment, Alice's Dad walked down the stairs into the living room. "C'mon, Al, get your coat. Nancy's truck just pulled into the drive," he said. "Hurry, you'll be late for school."

"See you later, Bobo," said Alice, hurriedly checking herself in the mirror above the couch before grabbing her coat and backpack and running toward the door.

"Hey, Alice," said Bo Parrot, "it's our secret, okay?"

"Okay, Bobo," said Alice, turning an imaginary key to lock her lips. "Our secret. See you later."

"Later, Alice," said Bo Parrot.

Turning on his perch like a skier changing directions on a slope, Bo Parrot looked out the window. The raven was still driving walnuts into the soft earth. Then the raven looked up from his work, took a couple of downhill hops and with a swift stroke of his wings was airborne.

Circling the meadow as he climbed into the cloudless sky, the raven passed so close to the window that Bo Parrot could clearly see a bright pinpoint of light reflected in his eye. He knew if he could freeze the moment and examine the raven's eye closely, he would find himself in the reflection. Then the raven sailed between the tall trees and toward the distant mountains. He was just a black speck when he was absorbed by the sky. On his perch, Bo Parrot beat his clipped wings uselessly. *He flies and I flap*, he thought to himself.

BARDWELL

CHAPTER 3

WHERE WERE YOU, BEFORE YOU WERE HERE?

Bo Parrot preened himself on the perch atop his cage as he did every morning, pulling each long flight feather through his beak, conditioning them for flights he would never take. Balancing on one foot, he stretched the other behind as far as he could. Holding this pose, he spread one wing over his outstretched thigh, like a fan dancer rehearsing a performance. Then he changed feet and stretched his other leg. As he held this pose, a soccer ball bounced down the stairs and slammed into the bottom of Bo Parrot's cage.

"Whoa! Watch it!" said Bo Parrot, wrapping his toes tightly around his perch as he bobbed and weaved to regain his balance. "I'm doing my yoga up here."

"Sorry, Bobo," said Alice, walking down the stairs.

"No biggie, Alice, you didn't do it on purpose," said Bo Parrot, vigorously scratching the side of his head with his foot, like a dog after a flea.

"I've been thinking, Bobo," said Alice, sitting cross-legged on the floor with the soccer ball securely in her lap. "The Solomon Islands are so far away. How did you get from there to here, anyway?"

"Well, my little flower, that's a very long story," said Bo Parrot, turning his head from one side to the other to get the kinks out of his neck.

"C'mon, tell me, *please*," begged Alice.

Bo Parrot flapped his wings, using the momentary weightlessness to reposition himself on his perch. "Well, it all started about thirty years ago, when I was hatched."

"Thirty years?" said Alice incredulously. "Wow, that really is a long time ago."

"I guess that depends on your point of view," said the parrot. "Age is a weird concept. The older you get, the more it matters. The younger you are, the less you care. Did you know some parrots live to be a hundred?"

"A hundred?"

"There are some macaws in South America who live that long," said Bo Parrot. "Some of the Indians there tattoo the design the macaws have around their eyes around their eyes, too. That's how much respect they have for the birds."

"Wow," said Alice. "I didn't know that."

"It's true. And if I lay off the table scraps and stick with sprout mix, who knows, I could live another thirty or forty years."

"Thirty or forty years?" said Alice. "Is that all?"

"Captive parrots don't live as long as wild parrots," said Bo Parrot.

"Oh," was all Alice could think of to say. "But, you seem sort of old already."

"You just think I'm old because I've always been in your life."

"I can't remember you ever not being around," said Alice.

"Well," said Bo Parrot, "I've been around longer than you know."

"Can you tell me more about the Solomon Islands, Bobo? I'm really curious," said Alice. "Did you live in the forest? Was it a forest like we have?"

Bo Parrot's blue and yellow tail feathers rustled like palm fronds in a tropical shower. "I lived in a forest, but it was a different kind of forest," he began. "All the plants had pointy leaves and it rained nearly every day. The air was hot and steamy. There weren't seasons like there are here."

"Was it summer all the time?" asked Alice.

"One long, endless summer," said Bo Parrot wistfully. "Our forest was alive with more animals and plants and insects than anyone could count. And everything was *huge*—ferns that you could sleep under, and dragonflies the size of curling irons."

"Wow!" said Alice. "As big as *curling irons?*"

"And the snakes, you wouldn't believe the snakes where we lived. Some of them had heads as big as oranges. Once a snake crawled right into our nest in the hollow of a tree. My sister and I freaked out and my parents screeched and squawked until he left. I'll never forget the look in that snake's eyes—yellow, slitted like a cat's, and hungry-looking. The snakes ate just about any animal they could get into their mouths—salamanders, frogs, lizards, rats, baby parrots. Lucky for me my parents harassed him into leaving."

"Actually," said Alice, unfolding her legs and leaning back against the couch, "I don't like snakes very much."

"Hey, don't bad-mouth snakes," said Bo Parrot, pretending to be offended. "They're distant relatives of mine, you know."

"I know," said Alice. "In school we learned parrots are, like, prehistoric, right? Aren't birds related to pterodactyls, you know, those giant flying lizards?"

"I think they were, on my mother's side of the family," Bo Parrot wisecracked. "Hey, check out my feet, see how similar my skin is to a snake's?"

"And your beak," said Alice, "it looks sort of like some of those dinosaur's mouths."

"That's another similarity," said Bo Parrot. "There's just no denying the old family tree. Anyway, our forest was a pretty amazing place. I remember ants with giant heads that swiveled around on their bodies as they hunted flies. It was like they had radar or something. They'd zero in on a fly and *Bam!* lunch time." Bo Parrot made a crunching sound with his beak to make his point.

"Whoa!" said Alice. "That's scary!"

"Especially if you were a fly," said Bo Parrot, allowing himself to be drawn deeper into the memory of his youth. "There was always something happening in the canopy. Hundreds of different kinds of arthropods lived on our tree alone."

"Arthropods?" said Alice. "What's an arthropod, Bobo?"

"That's what insects with segmented bodies and jointed limbs are called."

"Oh," said Alice. "You mean like beetles and ants?"

"Exactly," said Bo Parrot. "In our forest, you could never be sure about what you saw because things were not always what they seemed. I remember some spiders that looked exactly like ants."

"Spiders that looked like ants?" said Alice. "Why?"

"I remember asking one of my spider pals that same question and he said, 'So parrots like you won't eat us.' I thought about it a minute and you know, he was right—ants taste awful."

"That's pretty cool camouflage," said Alice. "Remember when I was a baby, Bobo, and I ate a spider? It was gross."

"I don't recall that, but I remember husking a sunflower seed once that was full of some kind of bug eggs," said Bo Parrot with a shuddering shake that started with his head and ended at his tail.

"Oh, yuk," said Alice, sticking out her tongue. "Don't even talk about it."

Bo Parrot gave a serene, Buddha-like nod. Then his voice took on a nostalgic tone as he recalled more details of his younger days. "Our forest was home to millions of plants and animals...it seemed to have a life of its own. Do you know what I mean, Alice?" said Bo Parrot. "It buzzed and hummed with the rhythm of life. One day I started thinking about all that life, all those plants and animals, all that incredible diversity and the way everything was connected to everything else—like one big party, one big dance."

"One big dance?" said Alice.

"Yeah, you know, like at Woodstock," said Bo Parrot. Then he began to sing. "By the time we got to Woodstock, we were half a million strong..."

"I saw the movie," said Alice. "All those naked people sloshing around in the mud...actually, it looked like fun."

"I guess you had to be there," said Bo Parrot. "Anyway, our forest was a wonderful place. Worms wiggled out of dirt that was piled a foot thick on the branches of trees. And there were giant weevils as big as your soccer ball, and each one had this little garden growing on its back—moss, ferns, all kinds of neat stuff. A weevil was a traveling salad bar that other insects could munch on. That's what I mean when I say everything was connected to everything else. If that weevil didn't carry that salad on his back, the insects that ate the salad couldn't survive. Any of this getting through to you, Alice?"

"Sure," said Alice. "Sort of."

"I remember a caterpillar that looked like a tiny dust mop," Bo Parrot said.

"Really?" said Alice.

"He was only two inches long," Bo Parrot said, then sighed. "Sometimes I wish I was a caterpillar, or a spider, or an ant, or a snake—anything but a parrot."

"But why, Bobo?" said Alice. "You're a beautiful parrot."

"Beautiful? What good is that?" said Bo Parrot. "Beauty only gets you captured and owned. It makes you into a *thing*. But let's not get started on that. Anyway, our rain forest was a place of great harmony. Life just sort of evolved without resistance, and there was a reason and purpose for everything."

For the first time, Alice heard about the rain forest from an animal who had lived there, and Bo Parrot's descriptions filled her with a sense of wonder. "What else do you remember about the rain forest? Did it rain all the time?"

"My next memory is very tragic," said Bo Parrot, a sad drift to his voice. "I'll tell you about it some other time."

"Tell me now," Alice pleaded. "*Please*."

"Maybe tomorrow," said Bo Parrot.

All this talk about the rain forest made Bo Parrot thirsty and he stepped inside his cage for a sip of water. He studied his reflection in the mirror above his water dish. "Some people say I look like John Lennon," said Bo Parrot in an English accent. "Do you think that's bloody true?"

At the mention of John Lennon, Alice began to sing. "Here come old flattop, he come groovin' up slowly..." Alice cocked her head and squinted at Bo Parrot. "Actually, you kinda do look like John Lennon. Your tiny eyes even look like they need glasses."

"I think I look like a cross between John Lennon and Mother Teresa," said Bo Parrot, studying his round-headed profile.

"Mother Teresa?" said Alice. "I don't think so."

"Come on, Alice, use your imagination," said Bo Parrot. "That's what it's for."

That night, snuggled in her bed, Alice dreamed of wild parrots streaking through the jungle, like rainbows chased by thunder. Downstairs, Bo Parrot listened to an owl calling in the night. "Whoooo...are you? Who who, who who?" the owl seemed to ask. But then Bo Parrot realized he was getting the owl's call mixed up with a rock and roll song playing somewhere deep in his mind, and he knew it was time for sleep.

BARDWELL

CHAPTER 4

A THOUSAND MONKEYS CLEARING THEIR THROATS

Alice's Dad stared at his computer screen, then looked out the window at the fog drifting through the trees. One tall fir, reduced to a silhouette by the billowing mist, was bent over at the top from the weight of the moisture. The top boughs suggested the head of a fire-breathing dragon—nodding and beckoning in the smoke-like fog. A splatter of rain appeared on the pane, then another, returning Alice's Dad to the present. Turning to his monitor, the words on the screen seemed to ask, "Now what?" Bo Parrot was perched on his shoulder and Alice's Dad looked at him out of the corner of his eye.

Just then a fly buzzed between Alice's Dad and the computer screen, and as it passed he swiped at it casually. To his surprise, the tip of his finger nicked the fly and it landed, stunned and dazed, on the desk lamp, which, with its sharp angles, taut springs, and cone-shaped shade, resembled a giant praying mantis.

Alice's Dad remembered reading about a man who had a friendship with a fly. The man could hold up a finger and his little fly friend would land on it. Alice's Dad's swipe had been a hostile, aggressive gesture and, thinking of this, he felt both ashamed and embarrassed. He wanted to apologize to the fly, if that was possible. Clearing his mind, he held an index finger in the air like a football player who has just scored a touchdown and projected good thoughts toward the fly. He saw the fly, who had by now recovered, buzzing in and out of the shadows. A moment later, the fly made a lazy loop over the keyboard, like a miniature crop duster spraying for vowels, and landed on the tip of Alice's Dad's finger. The fly seemed to be washing his hands, but otherwise, it didn't move, even when Alice's Dad held it up to his glasses for a closer examination. Holding his breath, he tried to focus all his energy on the fly, hoping the channels of communication would somehow miraculously open between them. He closed his eyes and tried to imagine what the fly would tell him, if it could. Would the fly recommend a favorite garbage can, or a particularly choice compost pile in the neighborhood? He was disappointed when there was nothing, just a black void, so he opened his eyes and stared at the fly, who was still scrubbing its hands like a surgeon preparing for an appendectomy.

"Check this out, Bo Parrot," said Alice's Dad, holding the fly an inch away from the parrot's beak. "Right there, on the end of my finger..."

Bo Parrot studied the fly on the tip of Alice's Dad's finger for a brief moment. Then, quick as lightning crackles across a dark sky, the parrot snatched the fly off Alice's Dad's finger.

"Hey!" said Alice's Dad, taken by surprise. "What did you do that for? That fly was a friend of mine." He studied the trace of fly left on his finger, a couple of well-washed legs and a bit of wing, then shook his head sadly. "We were going to be on Oprah."

Sorry, man. I thought he was a sunflower seed, thought Bo Parrot. *The old eyes aren't what they used to be. Alice is right, I do need glasses—fly-focals probably.*

Alice's Dad held up a finger and Bo Parrot stepped onto it. "Jeez, Bo, I can't believe you gobbled my fly. Really bums me out."

Bums you out? He wasn't exactly a gourmet's delight, you know, thought Bo Parrot.

"I think it's time for you to hang out with Alice for a while," said Alice's Dad, walking Bo Parrot into the living room.

"Bo Parrot's being a real wiseguy today, Al. He ate my pet fly," said Alice's Dad as Bo Parrot jumped from his finger onto the top of Alice's drawing easel which stood by the window.

"Your pet *fly*?" said Alice, looking up from her drawing. "What pet fly?"

"There goes my talk show career, down the drain," said Alice's Dad, shaking his head as he walked up the stairs.

"Did you really eat my dad's fly, Bobo?" Alice asked after her father had left the room.

"In the first place, it wasn't his fly—you can't own a fly. And in the second place, it was an accident...I thought he was a sunflower seed," said Bo Parrot, peering down at the drawing on Alice's easel. "Hey, what're you working on there?"

Alice stood back from her easel and regarded her drawing with a long-lashed squint. "A picture of the rain forest," she said. "Like it?"

"Very good," said Bo Parrot. "Is that a jaguar there in the corner?"

"It's an ocelot," said Alice.

"What's that pig doing in the rain forest?" said Bo Parrot. "Is he lost, or what?"

"That's not a pig, you silly parrot, it's a tapir," said Alice.

"I know," said the parrot with a clucking chuckle. "I'm just kidding you."

"Are you going to tell me the part of your story you didn't want to tell me yesterday, Bobo?" said Alice.

"Well, okay, but what happened next was very scary," said Bo Parrot, a dark mood settling over him like a veil. "Are you sure you want me to get into it?"

"I can handle it," said Alice, putting down her colored markers and sitting on the step. "I think."

"One morning, there was a new sound in our peaceful forest, a rumbling, rattling, *metallic* sound. We couldn't see it, but we could hear it, and we could feel it vibrating through the trees. It sounded like a thousand monkeys clearing their throats all at once. My father poked his head out of our nest and looked around. 'It's an earthquake,' he said. My mother guessed it was a volcano erupting on a nearby island."

"What was it, Bobo?" asked Alice.

"We didn't know, but we knew it was bad news. Then we heard tree trunks snapping like chopsticks. One after the other, *Snap, Crash, Snap, Crash*, the trees came down. Flocks of screeching parrots and cockatoos and lories filled the air, which had turned blue and smoky. A monkey poked his head into our nest and said, 'Flee for your lives.' But, of course, that was impossible for me. I was too young to fly."

"What did you do?" said Alice, both fascinated and frightened by Bo Parrot's story.

"My parents flapped their wings at the edge of our nest and screeched hysterically," said Bo Parrot. "They were afraid and confused—they didn't know what to do. Their fear made me afraid, too. I huddled with my sister at the bottom of our nest, but my curiosity got the best of me, so I pulled myself up to the entrance and peeked out."

"And?" said Alice with great anticipation. "What did you see?"

"There was fire and smoke everywhere; our beautiful rain forest lay twisted and broken. The roar of diesels mixed with the screams of thousands of terrified animals as they watched their homes and families being destroyed. I looked down and saw two giant yellow tractors with a thick steel cable strung tightly between them. They were *mowing* down our forest."

Alice drew a deep breath.

"Just like it was a lawn or something," said Bo Parrot, shaking his head with the memory. "Then the cable hit our tree and there was a cracking sound, and suddenly everything was tilted. My parents flew off as our tree started to topple, and I never saw them again. The vines, the twisted limbs, all came crashing down. Then I saw the ground rushing up to meet us, faster and faster and then..." said Bo Parrot, his voice trailing off.

"Oh, no," said Alice, burying her face in her hands. "What happened?"

"Our tree hit the ground and broke right below our nest, and I was tossed out like a feathery rag."

"What about your sister?"

Bo Parrot's green head drooped sadly between the bend of his wings. "She wasn't so lucky," he said.

"You mean she *died*?" said Alice.

Bo Parrot closed his eyes and nodded.

"Oh, Bobo! That's horrible!" said Alice. "What...what did you do?"

"Remember, I was just a baby and there wasn't much I could do," said Bo Parrot. "I couldn't fly—I could barely feed myself. So there I was, stunned, lying on my side, struggling to get upright and trying to be as small as I could so I wouldn't attract attention. Then, for the first time in my parrot life, I heard them."

"Heard what?" said Alice.

"The voices of human beings," said Bo Parrot. "I could hear them yelling all around me. From out of nowhere, a foot with a plastic sandal on it came down next to my head, and a hand came down like a giant spider and picked me up. A man held me over his head by the tips of my wings and yelled, 'Here's another one!' I saw the yellow tractors in a clearing. They were silent now, and perched on them so you could hardly see the yellow paint were hundreds of parrots and cockatoos. There was nowhere else for them to land."

For a moment Bo Parrot sat silently on his perch. A great sadness settled over him, like a deep shadow. He sighed and said, "That's enough for today, okay Alice?"

Alice sat stunned, a grim look on her face. Her lips formed a thin, down-turned line above her trembling, dimpled chin.

Just then Alice's Dad called from the kitchen. "Lunch time, Al. How about a little chicken salad?"

"Chicken?" said Alice, halfheartedly. "I don't think so, Dad. I'm not very hungry."

Alice stood and looked at Bo Parrot but his back was already turned. Lost in thought, he peered through the window at the rainy afternoon.

BARDWELL

CHAPTER 5

THE END OF THE WILD WORLD

Alice's Dad spooned a small helping of sautéed tofu, onions and green peppers on a saucer and placed it on the table in front of Bo Parrot, who was always pleased to be included in the family's dinner plans. His nails tapped the table ecstatically as he circled the saucer the way a second hand circles the face of a clock. He nibbled the tofu and then the pepper. After each mincing bite, he shook his head, scattering bits of food across the table. *Needs more garlic,* he thought.

"Bobo, you are one messy eater," thought Alice, her mouth full of pasta.

"Look who's talking," said Bo Parrot, splaying another mouthful across the glare of white Formica.

"I'm not as messy as *you* are," said Alice. "You're gross!"

"At least I have an excuse," said Bo Parrot in defense of himself. "There's no 'Miss Manners' for parrots, you know."

"Well, there should be," countered Alice.

"I only seem messy because I'm eating on this table where it's not cool to spill food. I mean, look at me dragging my tail across the table like this, trying to eat off a stupid saucer. You think this is a natural position for me?"

"Well, you don't have to be such a slob," said Alice.

"Slob?" squawked Bo Parrot. "Look, if I was sitting in a mango tree right now I'd be tearing mangos apart to get at the seeds, which is all I'd really be interested in, anyway. Most of the fruit would fall to the forest floor so other animals, like you, who can't climb trees, could eat it, too," said Bo Parrot, a little miffed. "And some of those seeds that fell in my so-called fit of bad manners would sprout and grow into new trees. That's one way the forest regenerates itself. Remember what I told you about how everything is connected to everything else?"

"Sorry, Bobo," said Alice sheepishly. "Sometimes I forget you're a parrot."

"That's okay. Sometimes I forget I'm a parrot, too," said Bo Parrot, shaking his head and scattering another beakful of food. "Hey, tell your dad to use a little more garlic next time."

As Alice's Dad placed a bowl of strawberries in front of Alice and dropped a single berry on Bo Parrot's saucer, Alice said, "Dad, Bo Parrot thinks the tofu could use a little more garlic."

"Oh he *does*, does he? I didn't realize Bo was such a connoisseur. Maybe we should get him a little chef's hat to wear," said Alice's Dad as he walked to the sink where the dishes awaited him.

"Tell him to get me a bib while he's at it," quipped Bo Parrot.

"And a bib, too," Alice called to her dad.

"A bib, yeah, right. Ha! A bib. Very good, Al," said Alice's Dad over the rush of water running into the sink.

"Hey Bobo, what happened after that man found you in the rain forest?" said Alice, biting into a plump strawberry.

Bo Parrot picked the seeds off his strawberry, one by one. "He tossed me into a burlap sack and tied a knot in it," said Bo Parrot. "A little light filtered through the holes in the burlap and I could see other baby parrots in the sack."

"So, where'd he take you?" asked Alice, dabbing her red-stained chin with her napkin.

"He slung us over his shoulder and started climbing over the fallen trees," said Bo Parrot. "It was rough going, and we bounced along on his back until he came to a pickup truck. He tossed us in the back of the truck and hopped into the cab. The door slammed and the motor started, and then we were rattling along a bumpy road. When the truck finally stopped, the man got out, untied the sack, and dumped us into the truck bed like we were a load of potatoes. Some of the baby parrots were dead from all the jostling around."

"Oh God, that's so cruel," said Alice, her dark eyes filling with a sudden gush of tears.

"Another man came by and counted us. He tossed the dead parrots into the bushes and put the rest of us in a crate," said Bo Parrot. "He gave the man who found us some coins and the man smiled. I was watching all this from inside the crate and I'll never forget that greedy grin—he only had a couple of teeth, like some kind of human jack-o-lantern. Then he nailed our crate shut. I'll always remember those wooden slats, the way they blocked the light, and the sound of the hammer striking the nails. It signaled the end of the wild world for me."

"The end of the wild world?" said Alice.

"And the beginning of my captivity," said Bo Parrot. "Anyway, then we were loaded into another truck with other crates stuffed with parrots and a few minutes later we were speeding along a highway. As we rode along, an intense struggle for survival went on inside the crate. The parrots at the bottom couldn't breathe and tried to wriggle to the top, but we were so tightly packed, moving was impossible. Fortunately for me, I was already at the top."

"Jeez," said Alice, blinking in disbelief.

"It was just starting to get light when we arrived at another place—an airport, I learned later. The man who was driving the truck turned us over to a man who was wearing a badge on his shirt—he was an official something or other. The man with the badge put some water and vegetable scraps in our crate, then lugged us into an airplane. I heard the airplane doors squeak on their hinges and then it was dark, darker than the inside of a nest on a moonless night. Of course with all the parrots jockeying for position, the water spilled."

"You must've been so scared," said Alice, losing interest in her strawberries.

"Scared? Are you kidding me?" said Bo Parrot. "I was *terrified.* We all were. I had no idea what was happening to me. My family was gone. My home was gone. Of course I was scared. Who wouldn't be?"

"What happened next, Bobo?" asked Alice, not certain she wanted to know.

"The airplane engines cranked and coughed and finally sputtered to life, and a few minutes later we were speeding down the runway. I could feel the tires hit the runway seams and then there was a strange floating sensation and I knew we were in the air." Bo Parrot paused to nibble his berry. "Man, can you believe that? The only flight of my entire life, and it's in an airplane."

"That doesn't seem...right," said Alice.

"We flew for a long, long time. It was hot in the plane, much hotter than in the rain forest even, and there wasn't much air," said Bo Parrot. "When parrots get hot, they spread their wings to cool their bodies. But we couldn't do that, and many more parrots died that night from the heat. I ate a scrap of lettuce and the water in that kept me alive.

"Finally, the plane landed—in Mexico City, as it turned out. Our crates were stacked in a rickety old shed near the airport with other crates of birds," said Bo Parrot.

"How many crates were there?" asked Alice.

"Hundreds, all packed with parrots fresh from the rain forest," said Bo Parrot. "A man wearing a mask and gloves sorted out the dead parrots, though it was hard to tell who was alive and who was dead. He tossed the dead ones in a wheelbarrow and some kid wheeled them outside."

"What did he do with them?" asked Alice.

"Buried them, I guess. I don't know, maybe he burned them."

"That's awful, Bobo," said Alice, cradling her chin with her palms, an anguished tone to her voice. "I had no idea this is how you got here."

"How would you know unless I told you?" said Bo Parrot. "But there's nothing unique about my story—this is how many parrots get to this country. Anyway, the tin shed was called the smugglers' warehouse, and we stayed there for a week. Each day more parrots arrived from all over the world—macaws from Brazil and Peru, greys from Africa, cockatoos from the South Pacific and Australia, Amazons from Columbia—every species you could imagine," said Bo Parrot, nibbling the last seed off his strawberry. "Do you remember what 'species' means, Alice?"

"Sure. It's a group of birds, or animals or plants, that have certain characteristics in common," said Alice. "Right?"

"That's right, Alice," said Bo Parrot. "All parrots have hooked beaks, right? And the way our feet have two toes that point forward and two that point backward? That's called, being zygodactylous. All parrots have feet like that. Different species of parrots have different characteristics, but some things about us are the same, and that's what makes us all parrots."

"Zygodactylous!" said Alice as if she was chewing gum. "What a word. I'd hate to have to spell that one in a spelling bee."

"It'd be okay—as long as you knew how to spell it."

"Well, yeah, I guess you're right," said Alice.

"Let's see, where was I?" said Bo Parrot.

"In the smugglers' warehouse," said Alice.

"Oh, yeah. Well, life improved a little in the smugglers' warehouse. At least we had food and fresh water every day. I thought the humans had a change of heart, but I learned later why they were being so kind."

"Why, Bobo?" said Alice. "Why were they?"

"Nobody wants to buy a dead parrot," said Bo Parrot.

BARDWELL

CHAPTER 6

A CARGO OF SHAME

Perched on the handle of a pitchfork in the garden, Bo Parrot looked a little like a hood ornament on an expensive car. Nearby, Alice sat in the grass and picked petals from a late-blooming daisy.

"He loves me, he loves me not," said Alice.

"Got anyone in mind, Alice?" said Bo Parrot.

"No," said Alice with a shrug of her shoulders, "not really."

"Well, if I was a boy, I'd be proud to be your boyfriend," said Bo Parrot, longingly.

"You would?" said Alice. "Thank you, Bobo. You're so sweet."

Suddenly there was a powerful whoosh of wind overhead.

"Listen, Alice," whispered Bo Parrot, scanning the sky with a wary orange eye. "Hear that?"

"Hear what?" said Alice, losing count.

Just then a raven glided into view over the tops of the trees. His ragged shadow passed over Alice and Bo Parrot like a low-flying plane.

Cawing loudly, the raven circled the meadow, then flew on. Bo Parrot sighed with envy and said, "Man, I wish I could do that."

"Fly?" asked Alice.

"Yes. I've never taken a flight as a free bird and it's been my one regret in life," said Bo Parrot. "At least in this life," he added, softly.

"Maybe you could fly with the raven," Alice suggested, hopefully.

"With these clipped wings?" said Bo Parrot, holding up his wings to reveal his trimmed flight feathers. "Get real."

"They'll grow out, won't they?" asked Alice.

"Only if your dad forgets to trim them," said Bo Parrot, wistfully.

"I'll bet the raven would like to fly with you," said Alice, trying to cheer up her friend.

"What makes you say that?"

"You're both birds, aren't you?"

"Yes, but he's a free bird, and I'm...not," said Bo Parrot, using his beak to pull himself from the pitchfork onto the wire mesh of the garden fence. He climbed the fence like a mechanical toy and eased himself onto a gnarly rosebush branch. White blossoms covered the thick, thorny bush and it hummed with the work of bees. The buzzing was so loud that Alice thought the rosebush might rise out of the ground, roots and all. Bo Parrot lost his grip and for a moment dangled upside down by one foot. He regained his footing and his composure and settled onto a low branch. His eyelids closed sleepily as he peered at Alice and whispered, "Hey, Alice, would you like to meet a friend of mine?"

"A friend of yours?" asked Alice, a puzzled look on her face.

"A parrot friend," said Bo Parrot.

"Where?" said Alice, looking around. "The only parrot around here is you."

"Well, he's kind of a magic parrot," Bo Parrot explained. "You can't see him unless you believe you can see him."

"*Believe* I can see him?" said Alice doubtfully. "Is he like Santa Claus or something?"

"More like the Easter Bunny, actually," said Bo Parrot.

"The Easter Bunny?" said Alice. "Sounds like a weird bird to me."

"Let's see what happens if we both use our imaginations," said Bo Parrot. "Let's see what kind of power we can generate together."

"Okay, Bobo," said Alice. "I'll try."

Bo Parrot drew a deep breath, filling his parrot lungs with the fragrant rose-scented air. He shook himself so vigorously that an aurora of parrot dust formed around his body like mist. Sunlight shattered the haze into many flecks of color. "Okay, let's go for it," he said tentatively. He'd never tried this before and wasn't even sure it would work. "Ready, Alice?"

"Ready, Bobo," said Alice, though she wasn't exactly sure what she was ready for.

Bo Parrot hunched his shoulders and pressed his orange beak deep into the down of his breast, so deep Alice thought he would puncture himself. When a white spot, like a tiny polar icecap, appeared at his crown, Alice's eyes grew wide. Slowly, the green began to drain from his feathers, and a few seconds later he was as white as a lime snowcone that had been sucked dry. His orange beak started to peel, the way thin bark peels from a madrone branch, revealing a gray beak as shiny and smooth as a wet stone. His amber eyes turned to little blobs of wet black ink and were surrounded by featherless white skin.

This new, strange parrot ruffled his thick, silky feathers and blinked, as if awakening from a deep, dreamy sleep. A crest, a white feathered pompadour with a blush of pink at the edges, erupted from the top of his head like a flower unfolding in slow motion. The crest gave the parrot the look of royalty, and made him look a little like Elvis. A sea of white roses, as brilliant as exploding flashbulbs, swayed around him like adoring fans.

"Hello, Alice," said the white parrot, his black tongue wiggling like a miniature finger from within the dark cavity of his beak. "My name is Kai."

"Hey...where's Bobo?" said Alice suspiciously, looking around the garden for Bo Parrot.

"Don't worry, Bo Parrot's still here," said Kai. "You just can't see him right now. It's all part of the magic."

"Magic?" said Alice. "I don't think I like this trick. He's coming back, isn't he?"

"He'll be back, I promise," said Kai. "But first he wanted me to tell you about something that happened in my part of the world."

"Something that happened?"

"Yes. Would you like to hear about it?"

"I guess so," said Alice, gradually warming to the calm demeanor of the handsome white parrot.

"I'm a Goffin's cockatoo. Twenty years ago I lived in a tropical rain forest on Tanimbar, which is an island in Indonesia near New Guinea, like the Solomons. One day men with tractors and chain saws invaded my forest, too, and cut down the trees."

"But why?" asked Alice.

"They wanted to turn the trees into chopsticks and souvenirs," said Kai. "They needed the money they would earn from these...these trinkets...to support their families. You see, Alice, people on Tanimbar are very poor."

"But lots of people are poor," said Alice.

"These people were poor and without hope. When they heard a Goffin's cockatoo sold for nine hundred dollars in the United States, they started to dream about the wonderful lives they would lead when they became rich from selling cockatoos. When our forest was cut down, the natives captured about nine thousand of us. They stuffed us in crates and lowered us into the dark hold of a junk."

"A junk?" said Alice. "What's that?"

"It's a kind of boat, Alice," said Kai.

"Oh, I know what you mean. The kind of boat with square sails that look like fans," said Alice.

"That's right, Alice, very good. Anyway, a few weeks later we sailed into Singapore harbor where we waited to be flown to the United States."

"That's sort of like what happened to Bobo," said Alice.

"It was a very similar situation," said Kai. "But between the time of our capture and the time we were to be flown to the United States, the market for Goffin's collapsed."

"You mean they didn't want the cockatoos anymore?" said Alice.

"There were already too many Goffin's in the United States and pet shops couldn't sell any more of us. So the Goffin's waiting in Singapore harbor were suddenly unwanted, which is a very bad thing to be. Our captors tried to persuade the Singapore government to let them release us on their island, but the government wouldn't allow it."

"Why not?" asked Alice.

"Because we weren't a species native to Singapore," said Kai.

"So?" said Alice.

"They didn't know what effect nine thousand Goffin's would have on their small island, and they didn't want to find out. So that left our captors with the problem of what to do with us. Returning us to Tanimbar was out of the question—it was too far and too expensive, and besides, where would we live? Our forest had been destroyed."

"Well, what *did* they do with you?" asked Alice.

"They took us out to sea and threw us overboard in our crates. All nine thousand of us drowned. It was the darkest day in the history of my species."

Alice was shocked, and her dark eyes brimmed with tears. "Oh, that's...that's...how could those people *do* that?"

"They could do it because we had lost our *value*, and were a problem to them. When human beings have a problem, they don't always think in the long-term," said Kai.

"Long-term?" asked Alice. "What do you mean, Kai?"

Kai ran a long white flight feather through his beak. "When you realize that what you do now may have an effect on the distant future—that's long-term thinking," he said. "There's nothing anyone can do to bring back us drowned cockatoos, but you can help make sure atrocities like this never happen again."

"But how?" said Alice. "What can I do?"

"You can help *educate* people, Alice," said Kai. "You can make them *aware*."

"But I'm just a kid," said Alice. "No one listens to me."

"But they *will*, Alice. You'll grow up before you know it, and you'll find people will listen to you if you have something important to say. You will *learn*, just like you're learning now," said Kai. "Pay attention to life's lessons and learn all you can. Then spread the word by sharing your knowledge with others."

Kai's feathers began to take on a green cast, slowly at first, then deeper and richer with each passing second. Feather by feather, his crest floated to the ground and became rose petals when they touched the earth. His gray beak gradually turned as orange as a piece of candy corn. A moment later, Bo Parrot, holding a white feather in his beak, reappeared where Kai had been perched among the roses. On the ground beneath him, Alice noticed, was a dark, wet stain.

Alice'
Garde
BORDWELL

CHAPTER 7

PASSING BLUE

With a hammer, Alice's Dad pounded a sign into the soft earth next to a tilled garden bed. "There," he said, stepping back from the sign.

"Alice's Garden," read Alice, with her hands on her hips. "Cool! It'll be fun to have my own garden."

"So, what kinds of vegetables are you thinking about growing this winter, Al?" asked Alice's Dad.

Alice thought for a minute and said, "Spinach, I like spinach...and some snow peas, and some broccoli, and maybe some artichokes and..."

"Beans," Bo Parrot whispered out of the side of his beak from where he sat on Alice's Dad's shoulder.

"...and maybe some beans," said Alice.

That afternoon Alice planted her seeds. After mixing compost into the soil, she created rows with her hoe, then poked holes in the rows with her finger and dropped various seeds into the holes. She sprinkled dirt over the seeds, then patted them gently with the palm of her hand.

"There!" she said when she was finished, brushing her hands together to remove the loose dirt. "All done!"

"That's definitely a good start," said Bo Parrot from his perch on the Alice's Garden sign, "but your garden needs a lot of care. You've got to water it, and weed it, and feed the plants if you expect them to grow."

"I know *that*, Bobo," said Alice.

"I know you know, Alice, but did you know that taking care of a garden is a lot like taking care of the earth? If you take care of the earth, and treat it with respect, the earth with take care of you."

Just then, the shadow of a hawk, as sleek as a jet fighter, passed over the garden. Bo Parrot watched as the sharp-shinned hawk landed in the shadowy boughs of a nearby fir.

"Uh-oh," said Bo Parrot, crouching low on the sign like a metal-flake-green, low-rider Chevy.

"What's the matter, Bobo?" said Alice.

"That hawk. He's hunting and I'm worried he might be tempted to try a little parrot sashimi," said Bo Parrot, trembling with fear. "Stay close, okay Alice?"

"Don't worry, Bobo," said Alice, shaking her hoe in the hawk's direction. "I'll protect you."

"Alice, remember last week when you met my friend Kai?" said Bo Parrot, secure now that Alice was close by.

"His story was so sad," said Alice. "It made me cry."

"There's another parrot friend I'd like you to meet."

"Another parrot friend?"

"Yes. He's very unique—a real one-of-a-kind guy," said Bo Parrot. "He's very sophisticated, very astute, a real gentleman among parrots. I think you'll like him. Let's see if we can get him to make an appearance."

"Well, okay," said Alice, a little apprehensively.

Bo Parrot fluffed his feathers and shook himself vigorously. With each shake he doubled in size and soon he was the size of a raven.

His small green primary and tail coverts flushed to a satiny indigo blue, and the furry green feathers of his breast suddenly became scalloped and turned a dusty, muted blue-gray. The blue-gray breast feathers held their color as they crept up his throat and around to the nape of his neck and gradually, feather by feather, turned as gray as thick billowing smoke from damp burning leaves. Bo Parrot's crown turned a lighter gray still, the color of ash around the edge of a dying campfire. The short green feathers around Bo Parrot's eyes scattered like grass clippings in the wind, leaving a mask of bare ashen skin. Quick as a blink, his orange irises changed to butter yellow and stared out intensely from the dark gray mask. The small pupils—piercing, pulsing black holes in pale yellow bubbles—suggested an otherworldly quality. Bo Parrot's mandible swelled like a bean left soaking too long and turned as black as tar. Just above the mandible, nostrils erupted like miniature volcanoes from the smooth gray mask.

Alice heard a tearing sound as Bo Parrot's stubby tail lengthened into luxurious plumage with feathers as long as sabers, cobalt-blue on one side, mink-brown on the other. Alice's eyes grew wide with wonder as Bo Parrot changed into the most elegant and beautiful bird she had ever seen, or could ever have imagined. The strange new parrot adjusted his stance on the Alice's Garden sign, checked to see that his tail cleared the ground, then regarded her with great seriousness.

"Good afternoon, Alice," he said, his voice thick with a Portuguese accent that was new to Alice's ears. "Please allow me to introduce myself. My name is Simon."

"Uh, hello, Simon," Alice said tentatively, awed by the parrot's strong physical presence and the remarkable transformation she had just witnessed. "What...what kind of parrot are you?"

"I am a Spix's macaw," said the parrot, turning his head in a slow, prideful way. "And what kind of little girl are you, if I may be so bold."

"I'm a...good little girl," said Alice because she could think of no other reply. "And I'm a friend of Bo Parrot's, too."

"I know," said Simon. "That's why I'm here."

"You're not from around here, are you?" Alice guessed.

"No, I'm afraid not, though I wish I was," said Simon. "My habitat is an isolated area—at least it was isolated at one time—along a dry riverbed in northeastern Brazil. For many years, our remote location was our refuge because our forest was very inaccessible. There were no roads and no foot paths. But, eventually, man found it and soon there were Jeeps and motorcycles and all that machinery," he added with a sigh. "You may find it interesting to learn that in the forest where I live, which is a relatively small area, there are 283 species of trees."

"Wow!" said Alice, who knew a thing or two about trees. "That's a lot."

"It is," said Simon, "especially when you consider that there are only seven hundred species of trees in the entire United States and Canada."

"That doesn't seem like very many for a whole continent, does it?" said Alice.

"Not when you compare it to the vast concentration of plants and animals in the rain forests throughout South America," said Simon.

"Your feathers are so beautiful," said Alice, running a finger along the length of Simon's tail.

"Thank you, Alice. Unfortunately, a lot of people agree with you and that's been part of my problem—that and the bees."

"The bees?" said Alice.

"The African killer bees that were accidentally introduced into Brazil thirty years ago. They were very aggressive and invaded many of our nesting cavities."

"For their hives?" asked Alice.

"Precisely. Soon there weren't enough sites left for us."

"Maybe that's why the Singapore government didn't want to let the Goffin's loose in their country," said Alice, remembering what Kai had told her.

"Possibly," said Simon.

"I've never heard of your kind of parrot before," said Alice.

"That doesn't surprise me. You see, I am the rarest of all parrots," said Simon. "Oh, there're a few Spix's living in zoos and a few more in private collections, but, in the wild, I fly alone."

"You mean you are the last Spix's macaw?" said Alice, not quite understanding how this was possible.

"I'm the last *wild* Spix's. When I die, my species will be extinct in the wild. When I die, and the few Spix's macaws in captivity die, our species will be gone from the earth forever."

"That's so...so wrong," said Alice, tears springing to her eyes. "No more Spix's...ever?"

"Only in books," said the Spix's macaw. "There is no recovery from extinction. It is worse than any plague, any disease, or any war. When it claims you, it is forever."

"But how did that *happen*?" said Alice. "Wasn't anyone paying attention?"

"Oh, people were paying attention all right," said Simon, "but only to their pocketbooks. You see, there were not many of us to begin with. Our range was very small, and we weren't, by our nature, prolific breeders."

"Prolific?" said Alice.

"We didn't hatch many babies," explained Simon. "And because there weren't many of us, we were in great demand by parrot collectors. Having a Spix's in your aviary was like owning a rare, expensive car, or belonging to an exclusive country club. As Bo Parrot would say, it's very *hip* to own a Spix's.

"As our numbers in the wild dwindled, our value to collectors increased—you know, the old rule of supply and demand. It wasn't long before a Spix's was worth sixty thousand dollars on the black market."

"Sixty thousand dollars!" said Alice. "Whoa!"

"Yes, a tidy sum for an animal wrapped in feathers," said Simon. "A couple of years ago, a poacher stole the last two Spix's chicks from their nest and sold them in Paraguay. Poachers aren't the most, shall we say, *aware* people in the world. I doubt that wiping out an entire species from the earth ever crossed their minds."

"They weren't long-term thinkers, were they, Simon," said Alice. "They should be ashamed of themselves."

"To say the least," said Simon. "But the so-called parrot lovers who create the demand for rare parrots certainly don't deserve any environmental awards, either. They're as much to blame for our extinction as the poachers, who are often just poor people trying to make a living.

"But I digress. As I have suggested, under the best of natural conditions, Spix's macaws do not produce many offspring. When our chicks were captured, few were hatched to take their places. The poachers took many adult Spix's, too, which reduced the opportunities to breed and reproduce even further."

"What about the Spix's macaws in the zoos?" said Alice. "Won't they breed?"

Simon chuckled cynically. "Spix's do breed in captivity, but only about thirty of us have been raised by aviculturists."

Alice bit her lower lip. "It makes me feel so helpless to know you'll soon be gone from the wilderness forever. Can't I do something to help, Simon?"

"It's much too late for me, Alice," said Simon. "But you can help. You *must* help. There are many other species in danger of extinction—not only parrots, but other animals, and other plants and other insects. Every one of them is important to the health of this planet, and who knows what secrets they hold? You and your friends can help by writing letters to your congressmen—tell them how concerned you are about the illegal importation of wildlife. Get involved, Alice, become a part of the solution. That's how you can help."

"*Involved*," repeated Alice, as if the word had just taken on a new meaning. "I will get involved, Simon, I promise."

"Let me tell you a story about—well, there's really no polite way to put it—how remarkably ignorant humans can be," said Simon, hopping down from the Alice's Garden sign to perch on the rock wall next to Alice. "A few years ago a parrot buyer came into a small village near the edge of our forest. He was looking for another kind of parrot to buy, a hyacinth macaw. A villager told the parrot buyer he had a young hyacinth that he had taken from its nest and was willing to sell at a very reasonable price. The buyer followed the villager to his hut where the hyacinth chick was kept in a small bamboo cage in a dark corner of the room. 'This bird is sick,' the parrot buyer told the villager when he saw the young bird. 'His feathers are pale, and his eyes are sickly and yellow. Look, he can hardly hold his head up.'"

"That poor little parrot," said Alice, sadly.

"The buyer did not want the parrot, and this disappointed the villager who was counting on the ten dollars he would earn from the sale to feed and clothe his family. The villager, who had risked his life to take the chick from its nest high in a tree, could see his sale slipping away and told the buyer he would sell the young parrot for only five dollars. But the parrot buyer thought the bird would soon die. He refused the offer and left the village.

"What the parrot buyer did not realize, of course, was that the bird offered to him for five dollars was not a hyacinth macaw at all."

"Was it a Spix's?" asked Alice.

"No, it was a Lear's macaw, one of the most endangered parrots," Simon said. "There are less than a hundred left in the wild. Like Spix's, they are the living dead. They, too, will soon be extinct."

Alice kicked the ground and shook her head in frustration.

"Had the buyer bought the Lear's chick, he might have nursed it back to health. A collector, or an aviculturist, might have bought it for many thousands of dollars," said Simon. "An aviculturist might, just might, have been successful breeding it. Sometimes humans beings aren't as smart as they think they are."

"What happened to the baby Lear's?" asked Alice, though she knew the answer.

"The villager did not know how to care for it," said Simon. "A few days later, it died."

Alice shook her head in dismay.

"There is a lesson to be learned from this story, Alice," said Simon.

"There are more people who want to own parrots than there are parrots to be owned. If humans continue to take parrots from the wild, what happened to us Spix's, and what is happening to the Lear's, will happen to other species, too. No living thing is immune from extinction. It happened to me, Alice. It happens to fifty thousand species of plants and animals every year."

"Fifty thousand! Every year?" said Alice, amazed at this incomprehensible figure.

"That's correct, Alice," said Simon with a slow nod of his head. "If human beings do not start living in harmony with other life on this planet, it could happen to you, too."

"To *me?*" moaned Alice. "Can't we *do* something?"

"It's too late for me, Alice," said Simon. "But, yes, there is something that can be done. Habitats need to be conserved, protected, and set aside forever."

"Why aren't people doing that?" asked Alice.

"They are, but it needs to be done to a greater extent," said Simon. "The beauty of conservation is that humans will never know how it comes out—or if it even worked."

"Why not?" said Alice. "It *seems* like a good idea."

"And it probably is," said Simon.

"It *feels* right," said Alice.

"It does feel like it is the right thing to do to keep the earth in balance. Conservation is a concept that needs to be passed from hand to hand, from mind to mind, from generation to generation. The same wilderness that you enjoy should be enjoyed by your children, and your children's children," Simon told Alice. "Can you imagine how wonderful it would be if humans could visit a colony of wild parrots in the rain forest and *observe* them without feeling they had to *own* them?"

"I've never seen a parrot living in the wild," said Alice, nodding in agreement. "It would be really neat."

"And it makes so much sense," said Simon. "Visitors would pay for the privilege of observing parrots in their native habitats. People in the host country could guide the tourists to viewing areas. Of course the tourists would need places to stay, and food to eat, and transportation. Wild parrots could be the cornerstone for an entire sustainable economy."

"That makes a lot of sense, Simon," said Alice. "I wonder why no one has done it?"

"They have, Alice. In Peru there is Manu National Park where visitors can watch macaws in their natural habitat. But it needs to happen in many more places—in Bolivia, Brazil, Zaire, Senegal, Thailand, Argentina, Paraguay—everywhere! The people who live in the rain forests need to learn that parrots are a resource and are more valuable in their natural habitat than in private collections. Bringing people to the parrots is infinitely more logical and responsible than taking the parrots to the people," said Simon. "Unfortunately, this kind of ecologically sound thinking is a lot to expect from certain human beings."

"But couldn't people *learn*?" said Alice. "Can't we *teach* them?"

"I can't teach them, Alice," said Simon, "but maybe you can. Maybe you'll be someone who makes a difference in the world."

"I will," said Alice with great resolve. "I will get involved and I *will* make a difference."

"I hope so, Alice," said Simon with a sigh, "but my time with you is almost over and I must take my leave."

Simon exploded off the rock wall like a pheasant flushed from a cornfield. His sudden burst of energy carried him to the top of a nearby fence post where he alighted and beat his wings with wild, raging fury. A haunting cry, full of the anguish and frustration of a dying breed, escaped his open beak and echoed through the trees, flushing the sharp-shinned hawk from his sanctuary. As quickly as it began, Simon's ritual was over. His body deflated, like a balloon with a slow leak. His blue and gray feathers turned algae-green and his black beak became as orange as a persimmon. His long tail feathers retracted into his body like a collapsing radio antennae to become, once again, Bo Parrot's stubby tail.

BARDWELL

CHAPTER 8

THE DANCE OF LIFE

Bo Parrot's wings flapped with each bouncing step as he rode Alice's shoulder down the old logging road that led to the oak tree. They poked along in no particular hurry, looking for salamanders under the rotting logs and damp rocks they passed along the way. But today there were only beetles and centipedes to be discovered burrowing in the moist decaying earth.

The logging road ended in a clearing. From there a path wound through a thicket of saplings, down into a ravine where the old oak grew out of a solid rock that formed part of the steep canyon wall. The rock erupted like a molar out of the jaw of the earth. Alice and Bo Parrot visited the old oak often. Most of the time they sat in the dry leaves and just looked at the tree, admiring its beauty and basking in the grandeur of its ancient energy. Of the thousands of trees that grew on their land, the old oak was special. It would take Alice and a half a dozen friends standing fingertip to fingertip to surround its massive trunk. Its canopy spread over the forest floor like an old umbrella; its branches, deformed by centuries of wind, twisted this way and that.

"This old oak is one amazing tree," Bo Parrot said to Alice, pacing the length of a young tan oak limb. "It's like a tree in the rain forest, the way it supports so much life. How many different critters do you think live in this tree, Alice?"

"I don't know," said Alice with a shrug. "A lot."

"Hundreds, maybe even thousands," said Bo Parrot. "See how the limbs have grown as they've followed the sun for hundreds of years?"

"They look like snakes," observed Alice.

"I love this tree," said Bo Parrot. "It makes me feel so, so *connected.*"

"Yeah," agreed Alice, getting comfortable on a mossy boulder. "It's a pretty cool tree all right."

"What do you think this tree is worth?" asked Bo Parrot, cocking his head to study the display of gnarled branches, each one covered with a miniature forest of tiny ferns.

"You mean how much money?" said Alice.

"Yeah, how much money."

"That's a hard question," said Alice.

"Well, you can't go out and buy one, can you?"

"No," agreed Alice. "You couldn't buy a tree like this."

"And you can't hire a carpenter to build one for you, right?"

"Don't be silly, Bobo," said Alice. "No one can build a tree."

"So if you can't buy one, and you can't build one, it's..."

"...priceless," said Alice.

"I mean, if something happened to this old oak, it could never be replaced." Just then a flutter in the top branches interrupted Bo Parrot's oaky reverie. "Hey, look up there!" said Bo Parrot.

"Where?" said Alice.

"There, in the top of the tree!" said Bo Parrot.

Alice squinted her eyes and looked to the top branches of the oak and saw a gray parrot peeking shyly from behind a curtain of bright green leaves, backlit by the afternoon sun.

The gray parrot cocked his head and said, "Is that you, Alice?" He hopped from limb to limb until he was close enough for Alice to touch.

"Look, Bobo, another parrot!" said Alice, turning to Bo Parrot, but Bo Parrot, of course, had vanished.

"What happened to Bobo?" Alice asked the gray parrot, her brows knitting suspiciously over her dark eyes.

"Don't worry, Alice, he's still here, but he's given me a chance to say a few words," said the gray parrot.

"Oh," said Alice, who should have been accustomed to such strange occurrences by now. "What's your name?"

"Jocko."

The gray parrot's softly scalloped feathers reminded Alice of fish scales. His short, blunt tail was as red as a vine-ripened tomato. The skin surrounding his pale yellow eyes was as white as soap. His black beak was as shiny as a flake of obsidian and his breast and wings were as gray as a cloud filled with rain. He was stout and solid—a parrot carved from stone.

"Where are you from?" asked Alice.

"West Africa, near the equator," said Jocko. "I'm a grey parrot. We're the most intelligent of all parrots, the cream of the parrot crop, so to speak. At least that's what humans think."

"What makes you so smart?" asked Alice, lying down in the leaves, lacing her fingers behind her head and resting it against a rock covered with moss as soft as down.

"I suppose it's our talent for imitating sounds."

"What kind of sounds?"

"Sounds like this," said Jocko. Then he made a sound like a barking dog.

"Wow! That sounds just like our neighbor's dog!" said Alice, sitting up suddenly.

Then a sound like an infant crying filled the air. It didn't seem like it came from anywhere, but, of course, it came from Jocko whose face was as expressionless as a ventriloquist's. "That's what you sounded like, when you were a baby," said Jocko.

"Did you know me when I was a baby?" said Alice.

"I've always known you," said the grey parrot, as if this was something Alice should have been aware of. "I can count, too."

"Really?" said Alice, picking three acorns from the nest of fallen leaves. "How many acorns am I holding?"

"Three," said the parrot. "And if you had three more you would have six. And six is the square root of thirty-six. Thirty-six times thirty-six is 1,296."

"You *are* a smart parrot, Jocko," said Alice, amazed at Jocko's mathematical wizardry.

"I can carry on meaningful conversations with humans, too," said Jocko. "But only when I'm in the mood, like I am now."

"What if you're not in the mood?" said Alice.

"I ignore them," said Jocko.

Alice laughed. "I like you, Jocko. Do you have a story to tell me, too?"

"I want to tell you about what life is like in my part of the world," said Jocko. "Kai and Simon are rare parrots, but we greys are still common in West Africa—even though thousands of us have been captured over the years and now live in cages as someone's beloved pet. But in the past few years, our flocks have been forced to find new forests to live in."

"Did humans cut down your rain forest, too?" asked Alice.

"Yes, just like they cut down Bo Parrot's and Kai's rain forests, but for different reasons," said Jocko.

"It seems like people are cutting down rain forests all over the world," said Alice with a sigh.

"It's sad but true," said Jocko. "Along the Ivory Coast, where I once lived, humans cut down mango groves that were hundreds of years old. Our flock huddled in horror and watched as they burned the fallen trees. Clouds of billowing soot blackened the sky, then fell to earth, covering everything, even the water in the rivers, with fine ash. Our beautiful jungle turned into a smoldering wasteland before our eyes. Humans may think grey parrots are smart, but the grey parrots think of humans as ignorant—too consumed with the present to think of the future."

"But why did they cut down your forest?" asked Alice. "For the wood?"

"For the meat."

"The meat?" said Alice, perplexed by Jocko's answer. "What do you mean?"

"You see, Alice, they wanted to use the land to graze cattle," said Jocko. "It takes a lot of land to grow enough grass to feed cattle, so they just kept cutting and cutting the forest until the land was cleared. Each time they came with their bulldozers and chain saws, the parrots and other animals retreated deeper into the jungle. More and more birds and animals had to live in less and less space," said Jocko. "As long as humans eat meat, they'll need to cut down forests to create pastures for their cattle. Think of it—there's just so much land—it can't hold out forever."

"But don't they know that's wrong?" asked Alice.

"*Wrong?*" said Jocko, with a shrill hyena-like laugh. "It doesn't even cross their minds."

"That sure isn't long-term thinking," said Alice, shifting her position to a smooth granite boulder.

"It sure isn't," agreed Jocko. "After a few years, the nutrients in the soil were used up, and grass would no longer grow."

"Then what happened?" asked Alice.

"Then the humans planted orchards, and fields of corn and beans."

"Bobo likes corn and beans," said Alice hopefully.

"Grey parrots do, too," said Jocko. "But when we came to the cornfields to feed, we were shotgunned out of the sky like ducks. And they laid out poison, too. I watched a hen nudge her poisoned mate all afternoon, trying to get him to fly. So we moved on, trying to escape the reach of human beings."

"People are so bad!" said Alice, exasperated, her voice full of frustration.

"They're not really bad, Alice—at least not most of them—it's just that they're not aware of the damage they are doing," said Jocko. "People in West Africa are very poor, and there's just too many of them for the land to support. They continue to have more and more children and don't think about the poor quality of life their children, and their children's children, will inherit. All they care about is their immediate needs, which is providing food and shelter for their families. They'll do whatever is necessary to survive, even if it means cutting down the forest and changing the balance of the earth forever."

"I know," said Alice wistfully. "I *know*."

"They've forgotten they are a part of the *process* of life," Jocko continued. "They've forgotten how important animals are, and the lessons that can be learned from them. A lot of people think, 'So what if a bird, or an insect, or a plant becomes extinct.' All they care about is making more room for man. What they don't realize is that animals are very important. They are part of the delicate web that holds the earth's ecosystem together. Man has to learn not to tear that web, just because he can."

"Humans sure do have a lot to learn," said Alice.

"The animals and plants of the world are humans' link to survival, Alice; they hold the key to the lessons for the future. People must learn that every living thing is connected to every other living thing. When a forest dies, the life and knowledge within the forest dies, too, and the lessons go unlearned."

"Like a book that never gets read," said Alice.

"That's right, Alice. You see, a forest that's alive with the chatter of birds and the grunting of animals and the unfolding of flowers is a healthy forest, one that needs to be preserved and protected.

"But when that forest is destroyed," Jocko continued, "the animals and plants must find another place to live, another habitat, or they, too, will die. Some of them, like Simon, become extinct. Every species on earth—humans, animals, insects, birds and plants—needs a safe, secure place to live. The earth belongs to no one species, Alice, it is a cooperative—it's for all life to share. Unless human beings learn that they are a part of the process of life and not the controllers of the process, life will end, just as it ended for Simon."

Jocko turned and climbed the old oak until he reached the top branch. He looked down through the tangle of branches at Alice and said, "Remember what I've told you, Alice. It's up to you, and kids like you, to change the way humans live on the earth."

Alice stood and yelled to the parrot, "But why *me*, Jocko?"

"Because it's *your* turn," answered Jocko from the top branch of the old oak, his gray plumage ruffling in the breeze. "Yours is the first generation whose respect for the earth is a part of you. You wouldn't throw an aluminum can into the garbage, would you?"

"Of course not," said Alice, somewhat indignantly. "I'd recycle it."

"That's what I mean," said Jocko. "Your dad's generation had to learn how to recycle, but you've never known anything else. The generation before your dad's never had a clue, and look at the mess they've made of things. And now we're all paying for their mistakes. But no one has to tell you what's right and wrong, Alice, you already know—it's a part of you. Make that knowledge work for you, Alice, make it work for all of us."

With a shallow downward stroke of his short wings, Jocko was airborne. Alice watched until he was a speck against the clouds. Suddenly he made a loop and flew back toward the big oak, as if he'd remembered something important. But the parrot that landed among the yellowing green leaves was not Jocko, but Bo Parrot.

That night a sound, like the faint buzz of an alarm clock in another room, woke Alice from her dreamy sleep. She pushed open the window above her bed and looked out at the night. The sky was salted with stars and a thin moon, the shape of a just-clipped fingernail, washed the meadow with a translucent milky glow. The sound was there before her, powerful but invisible, with a pulse of its own, rising and falling with each breath she took. She felt she could reach out and caress it. Alice squinted and could make out the shapes of deer grazing in the meadow, their yellow eyes glowing like jewels. And she could see the torn paper silhouette of mountains against the deep gray glow of the sky. She pushed the window open wide, and the sound entered her room and enveloped her. The voices of a million insects and frogs and birds that lived in the forest combined in a single joyous chorus. Alice closed her eyes and let the night magic fill her. She saw the creatures dancing and singing and leaping with the shared joy of being alive. *It's the dance of life*, thought Alice. With a serene smile on her lips, she snuggled beneath her blanket and her breath became a part of the chorus.

CHAPTER 9

WHEN A RANCH IS NOT A RANCH

Along the banks of the Eel River, the leaves of the maple trees that grew in the shade of the redwoods had already turned red and orange and yellow and hung like confetti caught in a spider's web. By this time of year the river had slowed to a trickle. The clear, deep pool beneath the cliff along the west bank was no longer deep enough for diving. Trapped by the low water, steelhead swam in endless, lazy circles, cruising for nymphs, pupas and late-hatching mayflies.

Alice and Bo Parrot sat on a snag that lay half in and half out of the water while Alice's Dad hiked upstream with his fly rod, hoping to convince a steelhead that the feather-wrapped hook he floated on the surface of the water was really a buggy morsel worthy of a quick snack. They watched, mesmerized by the graceful looping of white fishing line that splayed out behind Alice's Dad as he presented his fly, again and again, to the wary fish.

"I wonder what it is about fishing that people think is so cool," mused

Bo Parrot, as he sharpened his beak on the hard wood of the snag.

"My dad's been teaching me," said Alice. "It's fun."

"What's fun about it?" asked Bo Parrot.

"Mostly it's just fun being outside. There's so many neat things that you wouldn't see if you weren't fishing. One time I saw a bald eagle swoop down and snatch a fish right out of the river—it was amazing how he could do that. And trying to trick a fish into taking your fly is fun, too," said Alice.

"Seems like a lot of trouble to go through," said Bo Parrot, "just to outsmart a fish."

"Yeah, but it's really fun when you catch one," said Alice. "It grabs your fly and then it takes off with it."

"The old deception trick again," grumbled the parrot. "But this time the fish is the victim."

"They're not really victims," Alice protested. "When I catch one, I let it go."

"Why?" said Bo Parrot, curiously poking his head into a small cavity where a limb once grew from the snag.

"Because it's more fun to catch a fish than to kill it. If you let it go, the fish can go on with its life and make more fish, and maybe someone else will have fun catching it, too."

"If you say so," said Bo Parrot, unconvinced by Alice's argument.

"It's really exciting to feel them tugging on your line," said Alice. "It's like one end is attached to the fish and the other is attached to, you know, your heart, or something."

"Hmmmm," said Bo Parrot, gnawing at the edge of the hole in the snag. "The tug of life, eh?"

"Yes, that's *exactly* what it is," said Alice, happy that her thought had been presented so succinctly. She slid off the snag and picked up a flat stone worn thin and smooth by the rushing water.

"*I* get it," said Bo Parrot with a knowing nod. "You like feeling connected to the fish."

Alice skipped the stone across the surface of the water.

"Three," said Bo Parrot.

"Four," said Alice. "There was a little skip at the end."

Alice selected a few more flat stones to skip across the water while Bo Parrot followed his curiosity into the hole in the snag. Across the river, high against the cliff, a flock of ravens scolded each other as they swooped and dived along the sunlit bluff. Each raven cast a sharp shadow against the cliff which made it seem as if there were twice as many ravens than there actually were.

Alice looked at the birds wheeling above her and said, "What are those ravens so excited about, Bobo?"

"Youngsters learning to fly would be my guess," said Bo Parrot. "Flight school for the Raven Air Force."

"Flight school?" said Alice.

When Bo Parrot didn't respond, she turned to look at the snag, but Bo Parrot was nowhere to be seen. Alice walked to the hole in the snag and peered into its damp depths. "Bobo? You in there?"

"Just a minute," came a parroty voice from inside. A moment later a tuft of red feathers appeared, then a large, hooked beak, as white as ivory and as big as a wart hog's tusk. Alice stood back as the parrot's body emerged, trailing a long fiery red and blue tail, twice the length of her body. The parrot took a few pigeon-toed steps to a bare branch that was part of the snag, then, using her beak as a third foot, pulled herself to the top limb so her long tail hung unencumbered, like laundry on a clothesline. The parrot spread her wings. Banded with brilliant red, eye-smarting yellow, and deep-sea blue, the wings reminded Alice of a gaudy tie-dyed skirt. "Kinda cramped down there," said the parrot.

"Who are you?" asked Alice. "Another of Bobo's friends?"

"The name's Carmen Macaw, honey," said the parrot. "I'm a scarlet macaw from the jungles of Guatemala."

"Guatemala?" said Alice. "In Central America?"

"That's the place, child," said Carmen.

"Have you known Bobo a long time?" asked Alice, noticing the fine pattern of tiny red and blue feathers that lined the bare white skin around Carmen's eyes.

"All my life," said Carmen, "and that's a long time. Hey, girl, do you like riddles?"

"Riddles?" said Alice. "What kind of riddles?"

"Here's one I'll bet you haven't heard. When is a jungle not a jungle?"

"When is a jungle *not* a jungle?" Alice thought for a minute, then shrugged her shoulders. "I give up, when?"

"When it's a parrot ranch."

"A parrot *ranch*?" said Alice, a little confused.

"Never heard of a parrot ranch? Well that's not surprising, not too many folks have. It's kind of a complicated idea, so you've got to listen closely. Now, Bo Parrot's told you about how parrots are smuggled, right?"

"Yes," said Alice with a frown, recalling the details of Bo Parrot's journey to the United States.

"And he told you how badly parrots are treated in the process, so badly, in fact, that most of them die before they reach their destinations."

"*Most* of them?" said Alice. "Are you sure?"

"Well, nobody can be sure how many parrots don't make it because nobody knows how many parrots the smugglers started with in the first place, but trust me, hon, it's a bunch—a couple hundred thousand a year would be my guess. A lot of folks, bird lovers and conservationists, mostly, want the smuggling stopped. So someone thought up the idea of parrot ranching."

"So, what is a parrot ranch, anyway?" said Alice, leaning against the snag, looking up at Carmen Macaw.

"I live on a parrot ranch in Guatemala. If I took you there you'd see rain forest stretching out as far as you could see—prime nesting habitat for scarlet macaws, a whole bunch of different kinds of Amazons, and a lot of other parrot species. You'd look at the forest and probably say, 'Yeah, so what?' But what you wouldn't see is that the environment has been enhanced."

"Enhanced?" said Alice.

"Changed, manipulated—with food and artificial nesting sites. Imagine a patch of rain forest—it could be an acre, or ten acres or a hundred acres. This patch of forest—no matter how big or little it is—contains just so many hollowed out snags and trees for parrots to nest in and has just so much available food. Those two factors, plus the territorial instincts of the parrots, determine how many birds can survive in any given forest. But humans have come in and created additional nesting sites so more birds can live on the same amount of land."

"How do they do that?" asked Alice.

"Well, they take a length of plastic pipe, about a foot or so in diameter and as long as you are tall—you know, four or five feet. They put a plastic cap at each end and drill a hole in the side, big enough for a parrot to enter, about a foot from one end of the pipe. On the inside of the pipe they hang a metal ladder, so the parrots can have something to grab onto when they go in and out."

"And that plastic pipe's an artificial nest?" said Alice.

"That's right, hon," said Carmen Macaw. "The humans strap these pipes to trees, high enough off the forest floor so a parrot looking for a place to nest will find it and decide it will make a good place to raise a family. I mean, it's not as comfy and not nearly as organic as a hollow in a tree, but it'll do in a pinch."

"That's really high-tech," said Alice. "But what about food?"

"The humans plant fruit trees and vegetable gardens all over the jungle. Now, with plastic nesting boxes and plenty of food, the same patch of forest that supported one or two pairs of parrots can now support ten or twenty. And that's what's called a parrot ranch."

"Pretty incredible," said Alice.

"Naturally, having all these parrots living in such a small area makes the parrots easy pickings for poachers, so guards are hired to patrol the ranch, which creates jobs for the people who live there."

"What happens when they catch a poacher?" asked Alice.

"Poachers are dealt with severely," said Carmen, drawing a flight feather across her throat in mock horror.

"The guards also control natural predators, like the snakes and lizards and rodents who eat parrot eggs. They wrap sheet metal disks around the base of the trees so the rodents and lizards can't climb them."

"You mean like rat guards on boats?" asked Alice.

"You got it, doll. With conditions being so perfect, a bird ranch can produce a surplus of birds that can be 'harvested' for the pet market."

"But, is that *bad?*" asked Alice. "That's better than being smuggled, isn't it?"

"It's more *humane* than being smuggled, sweetie, but is it *better?* That's something we've got to look at very closely. See, this bird ranching business is a fairly new idea. A couple of years ago your government passed a law permitting the importation of 'ranched' birds. Just about all the environmental groups thought the law was a good idea because it would drive down the price of parrots and that would eliminate smugglers' incentives."

"So, if the smugglers didn't make so much money, maybe they wouldn't smuggle, right?" said Alice.

"Right," said Carmen. "Plus, the governments of the countries where the parrot ranches were could see the value in leaving the rain forest alone and wouldn't be in such a big hurry to cut it all down."

"Well, that seems like a good idea, doesn't it?" said Alice.

"It *seems* to make sense," said Carmen Macaw, "but as Bo Parrot has warned you, things are not always what they seem."

"What do you mean?" said Alice.

"Well, the whole idea is kind of like the fox guarding the hen house, if you catch my drift," Carmen continued. "See, the law also requires that these bird ranches, which are cropping up all over the world—in Ghana, the Ivory Coast, Thailand, Costa Rica, Peru—be *certified.* But certification is left up to the local governments, and that's where the problem lies."

"Why is that a problem?" asked Alice.

"Corruption, that's why—the temptation to make easy, illegal money. In many of these countries, the people are very poor. On the ranch where I live, baby birds, and sometimes eggs, are taken from our nests. That's what they call 'harvesting'. But each time a shipment of parrots or eggs is ready for export, smugglers show up with hundreds of wild-caught parrots that have been taken out of the wilderness. A bribe is paid to the government official who is supposed to be keeping a eye on things, and the wild birds are slipped into the shipment of ranched birds and no one knows the difference. The wild-caught parrots look the same and act the same as the ranched parrots. You know why?"

"Why?" said Alice.

"Because they *are* the same. In their hearts, in their souls, they are *all* wild birds. A bird that is harvested from a bird ranch doesn't *know* he's a ranched bird. I mean, he doesn't know he's been earmarked for pet status. As far as he's concerned, he's a wild bird, just as wild as the birds that are taken from the jungle. So, you see, darlin', this well-meaning law, in spite of its good intentions, gives smugglers a new way to smuggle."

"I see what you mean," said Alice, nodding her head. "Things really aren't what they seem, are they?"

"No, I'm afraid they're not," said Carmen. "But there is another issue here that we need to think about—an ethical issue."

"An *ethical* issue?" said Alice as a furrow appeared on her brow.

"This wildlife ranching concept is really nothing new," Carmen explained. "In Africa, they've been at it for years."

"Really?" said Alice. "What else have they been ranching?"

"It's more like *who* else," said Carmen. "In Zaire, along the Congo, bulldozers scoop out shallow pits in the earth. Those pits are flooded and filled with hundreds of crocodiles."

"Crocodiles?" said Alice.

"They writhe around in the mud and every so often the croc rancher tosses a wildebeest or gazelle into the pit and the crocs fight over it. When the crocs are big enough, they are harvested for their leather. Before they know what hit them, they're walking around New York disguised as a new pair of shoes, or a gaudy purse."

"So that's a crocodile ranch?" said Alice.

"Hey, have you ever seen those metallic blue butterflies they sell in import stores, sweetheart?"

"The ones in frames?" said Alice. "My mom's got some hanging in her bathroom."

"Ever wonder where they come from?"

"Actually, no," Alice confessed.

"They come from New Guinea," said Carmen. "The habitat is enhanced to produce an excess of butterflies, just the way the rain forest is enhanced to produce more parrots. Then the butterflies are harvested and they end up hanging over someone's sofa, or in bathrooms like your mama's—the ultimate insult if you ask me."

"And that's a butterfly ranch," mused Alice, shaking her head.

"In Zimbabwe, my dear, it's even worse," Carmen Macaw continued. "Wildlife ranching techniques are used to increase elephant herds."

"An *elephant* ranch?" said Alice, a trace of dread in her voice. "What do they do with the extra elephants?"

"'Hunting licenses are sold to so-called sportsmen. The license gives them the right to shoot an elephant at close range."

"That's...that's not *sport*!" Alice protested.

"It's like walking up to a cow in a field, pulling out a gun, shooting it between the eyes, then kneeling next to it to have your picture taken so all your friends could see how brave you were," said Carmen.

"That's disgusting," said Alice. "But what can we do, Carmen? How can we stop this ranching stuff from happening?"

"It's a tough one because it requires raising people's consciousness, and that's not an easy task, especially when there is money to be made," said Carmen. "Here's the question you need to ask yourself: Is wildlife ranching *conservation*, or is it *exploitation*?"

"Those animals are being *used*," said Alice. "That's not conservation."

"You're right, Alice, they're being exploited, and that's *not* conservation, no matter how much people try to convince you it is," said Carmen Macaw. "You see, if society thinks it is acceptable to raise crocodiles for leather, and acceptable to harvest butterflies for wall hangings, and acceptable to raise elephants just to be gunned down, is it acceptable, then, to enslave a creature as sensitive and intelligent as a parrot, an animal with a consciousness that rivals that of a human being?"

"No," said Alice, angrily, "not anymore it's not."

"Then it's up to your generation to draw the line that distinguishes conservation from exploitation," said Carmen Macaw. "Hey, let's face it, the human generation that controls the earth now sure isn't capable of making the distinction. They've proved that."

Alice threw a stone, but it sank without a skip.

"Here's the bottom line, honey," said Carmen. "Humans have a lot to learn from animals. Homo sapien is the dominant species on earth—and the species with the most *control*. And with that control comes a responsibility to maintain contact with wild animals. There are many lessons to be learned from them. They can teach humans to make responsible decisions about the future of the earth. Doesn't that make sense?"

"It makes a lot of sense, Carmen," said Alice.

"Then spread the word, hon, go tell it on the mountain," said Carmen Macaw. "Be a leader, show the way. No matter what you choose to do with your life, lead, don't follow."

"I will, Carmen," said Alice. "I know too much not to."

"Hey, look at those ravens up there, flying around light as the breeze," said Carmen, cocking her head, eyeing the swirling flock of ravens. "I think I'll throw a little color into the mix. See ya later, doll."

"Carmen, wait..." said Alice. But it was too late. Carmen lifted off the branch and with a few powerful strokes of her wings joined the ravens, who cawed all the more loudly at her colorful intrusion. After a few passes along the cliff, Carmen vanished over the grassy edge and became part of a small rainbow that bridged two fast-moving clouds.

A moment later Bo Parrot poked his sleepy head out of the hollow in the snag. "I must have dozed off," he yawned. "Did I miss anything?"

CHAPTER 10

BORN IN THE U.S.A.

The school Halloween party was just a week away, and Alice had still not decided on a costume. She discussed her dilemma with Bo Parrot as they lunched on the deck one warm Indian summer day.

"I could be either a Dalmatian, or a parrot," said Alice. "I just can't decide. What do you think I should be, Bobo?"

"Well, naturally I'm flattered that you're considering a parrot costume, but if I were you, I'd go with the Dalmatian rig," advised Bo Parrot. "All's you'd need is some white long johns, some black paint, and a couple of scraps of felt for ears."

"Maybe I could use my Goofy hat," said Alice.

"That could work," said Bo Parrot.

"Or maybe I could be a parrot, and *you* could be a Dalmatian!" said Alice, laughing.

"Me? A Dalmatian?" said Bo Parrot, imagining himself as a white parrot with feathery black spots. "No way."

Just then, the raven dropped down from the sky like a marionette on a string and alighted on the top rail of the compost bin. He looked around and, when he was sure he was safe, he hopped into the bin to pick through the fresh kitchen scraps for the choicest morsels. With a jerking motion of his head he choked down, somewhat cannibalistically, a scrap of chicken.

"That raven sure is making a pig of himself," said Alice.

"He's just being a raven," said Bo Parrot, still slightly distracted by the image of himself as a Dalmatian. "Ravens are scavengers. That's their trip. That's how they get along in the world."

The raven stabbed at an orange peel. He looked up suddenly, surprised that the peel covered his face like a mask.

"Look," said Alice, pointing at the raven and laughing. "The raven's wearing a Halloween mask...I think he's going to be a pumpkin."

"I didn't realize ravens celebrated Halloween," muttered Bo Parrot. "How bizarre."

"Bobo," said Alice, crunching a carrot stick, "what happened after your plane landed in Mexico?"

"One night, just after sundown when the sky was full of bats, a big truck backed up to the smugglers' warehouse and the crates of parrots were loaded into it and covered with a tarp," said Bo Parrot. "We bounced along all night and all the next day. The truck hit a deep pothole and one of the crates bounced off the truck. The voices of those parrots in the road will haunt me forever."

"Oh, no, Bobo, how awful," said Alice, wincing as she imagined the crate of parrots rolling off the truck and onto the pavement. "I'm glad you didn't fall off."

"I've been lucky that way," said Bo Parrot with a shake. "We finally arrived at a town across the river from Brownsville, which is a Texas border town. The crates were unloaded and stashed in a building with no windows—it was hot as an oven in there. No one bothered to feed or water us. A lot of parrots were sick and exhausted from weeks of mistreatment and confinement. Many of them just closed their eyes and escaped into death."

"But why didn't they give you food and water?" asked Alice.

"It's a mystery to me," said Bo Parrot, "because the closer we got to the United States, the more valuable we became."

"Remember that guy who picked me up in the rain forest?"

"Yes," said Alice. "The one with just a couple of teeth?"

"The jack-o-poacher," said Bo Parrot, keeping with the day's Halloween theme. "He was paid fifty cents for me, but once I crossed the border into the United States, I was worth one hundred and fifty dollars. When I finally made it to the pet shop—the retail level—I'd go for three hundred dollars, maybe more. That's big bucks for a bird, especially in those days. You'd think the smugglers would've been bright enough to take better care of us."

"You'd think so," said Alice, running the math through her mind. "So, then what happened?"

"Late one night we were driven a few miles out of town, to a lonely spot on the river where some teenage boys were waiting for us with plastic rafts, the kind you'd find in a supermarket," Bo Parrot continued, nibbling on a carrot.

"My mom had one of those, but it popped," said Alice. "She tried to fix it with fingernail polish, but the plastic melted."

"On the other side of the river was the United States. The crates were tied on the rafts with string, and all night long the boys ferried the crates across the river."

"That sounds dangerous!" said Alice.

"It was," said Bo Parrot. "I was watching from inside my crate and saw one of the rafts get away from the boys and float downstream. It spun around in the current and hit some rocks. Then the crate slid into the river."

"What happened to the parrots?" asked Alice.

"We'll never know," said Bo Parrot. "No one even bothered to chase them down."

"Oh my God, that's, like...like," said Alice, but she couldn't find the right word to describe the horror she felt inside.

"Like what it must have been like for Kai?" said Bo Parrot.

"Yes," said Alice, her voice filled with anguish. "It must've been horrible."

"Anyway, a truck was waiting on the other side of the river, and we were driven to a house near town and stashed in its garage. In the morning, a parrot buyer came by."

"A parrot buyer?" said Alice.

"He's the guy who buys the parrots from the smugglers," explained Bo Parrot. "And he's the guy who sells the parrots to the pet shops."

"Oh," said Alice. "Sure are a lot of people involved in smuggling, aren't there, Bobo?"

"A smuggled bird passes through many hands," said Bo Parrot. "Anyway, the parrot buyer pried open a couple of crates to check us out. He became angry and said, 'These birds are more dead than alive.' He was right, of course. Not having eaten for several days, most of us *were* more dead than alive. He argued with the smuggler about how much money he was willing to pay for 'this poor quality product', as he called us. They finally agreed on a price that no one seemed happy with, and we hit the road again."

"Where did you go this time?"

"The truck stopped at pet shops in small towns as we drove across Texas," said Bo Parrot, "dropping off a parrot here, half a dozen parrots there. My crate was the only one left when we finally got to the last pet shop, which was in a shopping mall in a big city. The driver waited until dark, then brought our crate into the shop through the back door and put it in a large, walk-in cage. He pried off the lid off with a crowbar and left us to find our own way out."

"Was that the pet shop where my dad got you?" asked Alice.

"Yeah," said Bo Parrot. "After what I'd been through, this pet shop seemed like parrot heaven—lots of perches and plenty of food and water. The cage was empty, except for a lone parrot perched in the corner."

"Was he from the rain forest, too?" Alice asked.

"He was this Amazon called Joaquin. I noticed a different kind of vibe about him right away—a sort of calmness that the other parrots didn't have," said Bo Parrot. "Want to check him out?"

"Sure," said Alice, helping herself to a stalk of celery.

"Maybe we can get him to pay us a visit," said Bo Parrot, hopping up to the deck railing. "But to do that, we have to lure him into our consciousness by singing a special song."

"What kind of special song?" said Alice.

"A Mexican song," said Bo Parrot. He started to sing. "*La cucaracha, la cucaracha, yo no puedo caminar. La cucaracha, la cucaracha, yo no puedo caminar*... Come on, Alice, sing with me."

"*La cucaracha, la cucaracha, yo no puedo caminar*," sang Alice. "*La cucaracha, la cucaracha, yo no puedo caminar*..."

As Bo Parrot sang, he danced a pigeon-toed, avian cha-cha—one, two, one, two, three—stumbling to the Latin beat Alice pounded out on the table top with her spoon. Bo Parrot twirled and whirled at a reckless, dizzying pace while singing at the top of his lungs. Just as Alice feared the momentum of his dance would hurl him from the deck railing to an uncertain fate, he slowed down, wobbling like a top that has lost its spin. He staggered to regain his balance, and Alice saw he no longer resembled Bo Parrot.

"Whoa, Nelly!" said the parrot, spreading his toes and touching his wing tips to the railing to steady himself. "*Hola, muchacha!* You must be that little Alice *chiquita El* Bo told me about."

"Elbow?" said Alice.

"No, *El* Bo—it's a Spanish expression of respect—like *Mister Bo*. Anyway, *Me llamo Joaquin. A sus ordines*," the parrot said, folding a wing behind him, in an awkward, comical bow.

"You're not Joaquin," said Alice, laughing at the wobbling parrot. "You're Bobo!"

"Well, maybe so," said Joaquin. "But I am Joaquin, too. I'm also hungry. Those carrots sure look good."

"They're from my garden," said Alice, pushing the plate to the center of the table. "Have all you want. Carrots are good for your eyes."

"Is that so?" said Joaquin, doubtfully. "Rabbits are big carrot eaters, aren't they?"

"Yes," agreed Alice. "Carrots are their favorite food."

"Then how come you see so many rabbits run over on the highway? You'd think they would've seen the cars coming and hopped out of the way."

Alice was perplexed by the truth of this observation, and stared at the raven who was trying to dislodge the orange peel from his beak by rubbing it against the frame of the compost bin.

Joaquin jumped onto the table, waddled to the edge of Alice's plate and took a bite of carrot. "You're probably wondering what tale of woe I'm going to tell you," he said.

"All of Bobo's friends told me stories about what happened to them," said Alice. "They were all sad stories, but I learned a lot."

"Sad stories often have a lesson or two in them," said Joaquin. "But my story is different; my story's got a happy ending."

"That's good," said Alice. "Those other stories really made me sad for the parrots. Hey, are you really an Amazon parrot?"

"A Blue-fronted Amazon, to be precise," said Joaquin, leaning toward Alice so she could clearly see the colorful distribution of feathers on his head. "Check out my stylish, ultra-cool do—is it hip, or what?"

"You look like a rock star," said Alice, running her index finger lightly over the short blue fuzz of feathers just above Joaquin's beak. "Are you from the rain forest, too?"

"Rain forest? What do I know from rain forests?" said Joaquin. "I was hatched and raised in an aviary, right here in the U. S. of A."

"So, you don't know anything about rain forests?" asked Alice.

"I've never been to a rain forest in my life—you know more about rain forests than I do. I'm what's called a domestic parrot," said Joaquin. "And, like all domestic parrots, I'm kind of an orphan. I never knew my real parents."

"Really?" said Alice. "Why not?"

"My parents, who once were wild birds like Kai and Jocko, live in a flight in an aviary."

"A flight?" said Alice. "What's that?"

"It's a cage that is long enough for a parrot to fly from one end to the other in about two seconds—which is not that great but it's better conditions than a lot of parrots live in."

"Oh, Bobo's got one of those," said Alice. "I didn't know it was called a flight."

"It's comfortable and it's secure from predators, you know, ring-tail cats, hawks, raccoons, coyotes—your basic parrot munchers. Anyway, let me tell you how I got to be a domestic parrot."

"Okay," said Alice. "I'd like to hear about that."

"Well, one day an egg is laid in the nesting box. As soon an egg is laid, the aviculturist—he's the guy who takes care of the parrots living in the aviary—puts it in an incubator where it's got a good chance of hatching."

"Why can't the mother parrot hatch the egg herself?" asked Alice.

"Just because a breeder parrot is good at laying eggs doesn't mean she's good at hatching them. The egg could be accidentally broken by an inexperienced hen who doesn't know what she's doing," Joaquin explained. "Anyway, a month or so later, *Voila!*, I hatch! I am coaxed out of my shell by a human being who feeds me a nutritious mixture every few hours. I'm kept safe and warm in a plastic box with washcloths rolled up along the inside walls."

"What are the washcloths for?" asked Alice.

"They're bumpers so I don't hurt myself when I'm rolling around in the box like a rubber ball," said Joaquin.

"A rubber ball?" said Alice.

"Baby parrots are pretty weird looking little creatures," said Joaquin. "A few weeks later my eyes open and the first thing I see is this mysterious human being creature. Since I have no idea what I look like or that I'm even a parrot, I naturally think this human is my parent. It doesn't occur to me that maybe he is not. So, I imprint on this human being who takes care of me. The weeks go by and I grow stronger and soon I fledge."

"Fledge?" said Alice, fascinated by Joaquin's story. "Is that when you start to get feathers?"

"No, fledging is when a parrot is ready to leave the nest," Joaquin explained. "Anyway, so there I am, living the good life in the aviary nursery with other baby parrots. There is a big playpen outside where the young parrots—we're like teenagers by now..."

"I'll be one soon, too," Alice put in.

"Yeah? Well, congratulations, and just remember, those zits are only temporary. Anyway, we hang out in the playpen during the day. Our human caretakers play with us and at night they return us to the nursery. We like our caretakers. Secretly, we wish we could stay with them forever, which, to a baby parrot, is like what happens in the next few minutes. But one day, we wake up and we're fully feathered and eating on our own, and it's time to leave the aviary."

"Yeah, I know. They've got to sell you to somebody in Idaho or somewhere, right?" said Alice.

"Or a pet store somewhere," said Joaquin. "Some human being out there in the world needs me. You see, Alice, human beings *like* parrots. If you ask someone why he has a pet parrot, he'll probably tell you it's because they are so beautiful and colorful, but that's not really why people keep parrots."

"Then what *is* the real reason?" asked Alice.

"A parrot kisses you and cuddles with you and rolls over and *talks*...talks to you in your own language! Name one other animal that does that?"

"I can't think of any," said Alice.

"Well, there aren't any, and that's what makes us unique and so irresistible. Getting that kind of attention and intelligence from such an exotic creature—like, ahem, *moi*—is a fascinating experience for humans," said Joaquin. "You see, parrots have the *scent* of wildness, and humans pick up on it."

"Even parrots that are hatched in the aviary?" asked Alice. "They have that wild scent, too?"

"Sure they do," said Joaquin. "Remember, most parrots that are hatched in an aviary are only a generation or two out of the jungle. That connection to the wilderness, that *parrotness*, is still a part of them."

"Kind of like a stain that won't come out of a skirt?" asked Alice.

"Well, sort of like that, yeah," said Joaquin. "Humans like being connected to parrots, and the parrots *know* they like it. They tune into what the humans need, and respond with love and adoration. Most humans don't even know it, but they keep parrots because they like the way a parrot makes them *feel*. The unconditional love a parrot gives a human is a lot like the unconditional love a child gives her parent."

"I guess that's why I love Bobo so much," said Alice. "He's my best friend."

"People who keep pet parrots consider themselves bird lovers," said Joaquin. "Unfortunately, many of them don't stop to think where a lot of the parrots they love so much come from, or how much they have suffered to become their pets."

"You mean like what happened to Bobo?" said Alice.

"That's right, Alice, like what happened to *El* Bo and tens of thousands of parrots just like him," said Joaquin. "You see Alice, bird lovers create the *demand* for parrots. They don't realize it, but they are the reason that a man in Mexico, or Brazil, or Zaire, climbs a tree and steals a baby parrot from its nest."

"They're not very aware, are they, Joaquin?" said Alice, wrinkling her nose.

"A bird lover who buys a wild-caught parrot is as just guilty as the smugglers are for the suffering a parrot goes through," said Joaquin. "People who want a pet parrot should buy a parrot like me, one born and raised in captivity, not one taken from his jungle home and kept prisoner for the rest of his life."

"But I don't think my dad knew Bobo was a smuggled parrot when he bought him," said Alice.

"He probably didn't," said Joaquin. "He probably didn't even think about where *El* Bo came from. You see, Alice, parrots have feelings and memories. When a parrot is taken from the wild, he remembers what it was like to be free. Even though he is confined to a cage, he is *still* a wild bird, and he can never really forget that he was once free."

"Bobo told me he would like to fly like a free bird," said Alice.

"I'm sure he would," said Joaquin. "Do you know what the main difference between a wild-caught parrot and a captive-bred parrot is?"

"What?" said Alice.

"A captive-bred parrot goes willingly into a home to become part of a human family. A cage is nothing new to him. He looks at a cage like it's his own private space," said Joaquin.

"Like my bedroom is to me?" said Alice.

"Exactly, like your bedroom, Alice," said Joaquin. "Living with humans is the only life I have ever known. If I make a human happy, I'm happy. It's my job. It's how I *want* to live; it's how I *must* live," said Joaquin, crunching a carrot stick. "Uh-oh, you know what, Alice?"

"What?" said Alice.

"I'm getting that Bobo feeling again," said Joaquin. "It's been fun chatting with you, but it's time for me to get on down the road. Hasta la bye-bye, as they say south of the border."

"Hasta la bye-bye, Joaquin," said Alice.

Joaquin held out his wings and started spinning like a well-thrown Frisbee, faster and faster, until he was a green blur. His momentum spun him off the table and onto the floor. When Alice looked down to see if he was all right, it was Bo Parrot who peered sheepishly up at her. "Smoke and mirrors, Alice," he said with a wink of his mischievous orange eye.

CHAPTER 11

THE MYSTERY OF THE DISTANCE

On a morning when the valleys between the ridge tops were filled with fog but the sky above them was clear, Alice and Bo Parrot worked on a rain forest puzzle that was laid out on the glass coffee table in the living room.

"I'm looking for the jaguar's ear," said Alice, on her knees, leaning over the table.

"I'm looking for the macaw's ear," said Bo Parrot, his nails tapping the glass impatiently.

"Silly parrot," scolded Alice. "Macaws don't have ears."

"All parrots have ears," said Bo Parrot. "You just can't see them because they're covered by feathers."

"I *knew* that," said Alice.

"That's what I heard," said Bo Parrot, with a cluck and a chuckle.

While Alice looked for the jaguar's ear, a flash of black, like sunlight glinting off a piece of shiny black satin, caught Bo Parrot's eye. He glanced into the mirror above the couch and watched the reflection of the raven land in the walnut tree. As the raven tucked his inky wings into his body, he seemed to look at Bo Parrot. He cawed loud and throaty. Bo Parrot cocked his head. *Is he talking to me?* he thought. *He can't see me through the window, can he?* Bo Parrot watched the raven hop from branch to branch examining the speckled green pods. The raven cocked his head and again seemed to stare at Bo Parrot. *Caw-caw-caw-caw.* Bo Parrot's orange eye began to pulse excitedly. He knew his time had come.

"Alice," said Bo Parrot, "let's talk a minute, okay?"

"Okay, Bobo," said Alice, putting the jaguar's ear in its place.

"These past few weeks I've told you about my life's journey. You've met some of my parrot friends—Kai, Simon, Jocko, Carmen, Joaquin—and they've told you their stories, too. I hope you've learned that the cutting down of rain forests and the destruction of wildlife habitat is not something that is happening in just one part of the world."

"It's happening all over," said Alice with a deep sigh.

"And I hope you've learned that wild things are best left in the wilderness."

"I've learned a lot from you and your parrot friends, Bobo," said Alice.

"That's good," said Bo Parrot, a serious, somber tone to his voice, "because you, and kids like you, will determine what happens next, not only to parrots, but to every other living thing on earth. It's a huge responsibility. Do you think you're up to it, Alice?"

"Definitely, Bobo," said Alice, confidently.

"That's good, Alice," said Bo Parrot, "because nothing is more important than taking care of the earth. It's the only home you and the rest of us will ever have."

"I'll do my best to take care of it, Bobo."

"Promise?"

"Promise."

"I love you, Alice."

"I love you, too, Bobo."

"I'll always be with you. Even if you can't see me, I'll be with you."

"You're with me right now," said Alice.

"But even if I'm not here, even if you can't see me, my spirit will be with you," said Bo Parrot. "You'll be able to feel me inside you, all you have to do is listen to your heart."

"Listen to my heart?" said Alice.

"Your heart will lead you," said Bo Parrot, "but you have to listen."

"Will you still be able to talk to me, even if you're not here?" asked Alice, a worried tone to her voice.

"Of course," said Bo Parrot. "Always."

Alice and Bo Parrot stared at each other over the partially completed rain forest puzzle. Then Bo Parrot began to flap his wings, slowly at first, and then faster and faster. Loose puzzle pieces scattered to the floor with the turbulence created by his wings. Suddenly he lifted off the table and flew over Alice's head and into the mirror hanging above the couch. He passed through the reflection, as easily as a coin passes through the surface of the water in a wishing well, and landed next to the raven in the walnut tree. Bo Parrot held his wings over his head like a prize fighter who has just scored a knockout punch, his flight feathers fully restored. "I'm free, Alice!" Bo Parrot called from the silvery depths of the mirror, his triumphant voice a faraway echo, "I'm finally *free*!"

The raven spread his wings and leaped into the air. A strong downward stroke initiated a glide that carried him over the garden and toward the mountains. In the distance, mist rolled and swirled in the valleys like smoke from a fire. The pointy ridge tops above the mist looked like castle silhouettes rising out of a foggy sea.

Bo Parrot, confident now in his own powers of flight, followed the raven, his short wings beating faster and faster to close the gap between himself and the graceful black bird. Oh, how long he had waited to feel the lift of freedom beneath his wings! How wonderful it felt! He flew higher and faster, over the garden, banking between the tall firs, into the mystery of the distance. "I'm free, Alice, I'm finally free!" called Bo Parrot from the edge of the sky.

Mesmerized, Alice stared into the mirror and watched until the two birds were enveloped by the mist. She put her hand to the mirror and was amazed when it, too, passed easily into a reality where all birds were free. Her fingers felt warm and cool at the same time, and her cheeks burned with excitement. Then she turned and looked out the window at the walnut tree. A breeze moved through the leaves, but the raven and Bo Parrot were gone.

CHAPTER 12

I ONCE HAD A PARROT...

The country school Alice attended overlooked a large meadow. Visible through the classroom window was the vegetable garden the children tended and an apple orchard. In many ways the little schoolhouse, with its garden and sweeping vistas, reminded Alice of her own hillside home.

Just before Thanksgiving, a few weeks after Bo Parrot's flight to freedom, Alice's class began to study the rain forests of the world. The students learned about the animals and plants that lived in the rain forests, and how necessary rain forests were to the health of the planet. They learned that the cures to many diseases—diseases like cancer, leukemia and AIDS—might come from the plants that grew in the rain forests. They also learned that rain forests all over the world were being razed at an alarming rate, an acre every minute in some places. Some of the medicinal plants, Alice's teacher told the class, might become extinct before they were discovered.

One of the assignments Alice's teacher gave the class was for the children to write a story about an animal that lived in the rain forest, an animal that was special to them. The students would read their stories at a special presentation to be made to the parents and other children who attended the school.

The classroom was packed on the day of the students' rain forest presentations. Each child stood at a podium at the front of the class and read their stories to their classmates and the parents who had come to listen. Louise read her story about the jaguar, and Adam read his about the howler monkey. When Bekah finished her story about the peccary, it was Alice's turn to read.

Alice walked to the front of the room, clutching her notebook tightly against her chest. She looked at the audience. Her classmates, her teachers, the parents of her friends and her father waited to hear her story. Her eyes were bright with excitement and her heart raced nervously. She drew a deep breath and the audience hushed. Then, Alice saw a raven land in an apple tree outside the classroom window. No one else saw it because everyone was looking at her. Then, another bird landed in the tree, flapping his short green wings awkwardly to keep his balance. Alice smiled and felt her heart calm. The door at the back of the room opened quietly and a tall, dark-skinned boy wearing a New York Yankees T-shirt stepped inside and stood quietly against the wall. He looked at Alice and smiled. Alice looked at him for a long moment, then acknowledged him with a smile and a slight nod of her head. She opened her notebook. "I once had a parrot named Bobo," she began, "and he taught me the dance of life..."

BARDWELL

POSTSCRIPT

THE MESSAGE AND THE MESSENGER

Earlier today, with Bo Parrot perched on my shoulder while I sat at my computer writing this story, a strange feeling came over me. Until now, I thought I had been writing a story about parrots, a story I hoped Alice, and children like Alice, would read, or have read to them. I hoped the story would influence the way the children thought about parrots and their relationship to the world of human beings. I hoped the children who read *What the Parrot Told Alice* would evolve into people who would strive to make a difference in the world, who would become tomorrow's caretakers and protectors of the earth. The story was my song to sing in a world desperately in need of harmony.

Until now, until this moment of clarity, I thought I was making the story up. I thought that I, and I alone, created the fantasy and imagined the dialogue between Alice and Bo Parrot and the other parrots in the story. But now, with Bo Parrot nuzzling my beard, and as I feel the warm charge of energy pass between us, I am not so sure. The words that formed the story came from somewhere, but I am no longer certain they have sprung from my own creative resources.

Now Bo Parrot cocks his feathery green head and stares me down, his dark pupils pulsing within his orange irises like a total eclipse of the sun. He coos softly and pulls at my hair. Bo Parrot's turned on, I think, but what is he turned on about? Then it comes to me, as clear and focused as a forest dripping with rain: Bo Parrot is turned on by the *process*. The story is almost told, and he, Bo Parrot, has been successful in his effort to merge his parrot consciousness with my human consciousness. Bo Parrot is excited because his story and the story of parrots around the world has been told to someone who will pass along its truth to people who need to know.

As I connect with the reason for Bo Parrot's joy, my understanding of my role in the telling of the story becomes clear as well. *What the Parrot Told Alice* is not my story to tell. It never has been. I didn't make it up, I didn't create it, and it isn't fiction. I didn't even write it, I only wrote it down. It really happened, every word of it, and I finally understand that I am the medium, but the message is clearly Bo Parrot's.

Dale Smith

Dale Smith
February 7, 1996

GLOSSARY

SOME NOT-SO-COMMON WORDS

CHAPTER 1

lap-lap

a skirt tied around the waist

Siwai

a tribe of people on the island of Bougainville, formerly in the Solomon Islands, but now a part of Papua New Guinea

Solomon Islands

a chain of 992 islands, atolls and cays in the South Pacific Ocean near Papua New Guinea

CHAPTER 2

mango

a tart, juicy tropical fruit with a thick, reddish rind

metronome

an instrument that makes repeated clicks for marking rhythm

Papua New Guinea

an island nation in the South Pacific Ocean

periwinkle

a trailing perennial with blue-violet flowers

plumage
feathers of a bird
Robert DeNiro
an actor known for his line in the movie *Taxi Driver*, "You talkin' to me?"

CHAPTER 3

arthropods
insects with segmented bodies
bloody
an expression used by the British
camouflage
to reduce the visibility of an object by disguise
harmony
agreement, amity, accord
John Lennon
one of the Beatles, killed by a gunman in 1980
Mother Teresa
a nun known for her work with the poor in Calcutta, India
nostalgic
homesick
pterodactyl
prehistoric winged lizard of the dinosaur family
Woodstock
a 1969 rock concert and gathering of 500,000 hippies in upstate New York

---

CHAPTER 4

appendectomy
a surgical operation for removal of the appendix
gourmet
a connoisseur of food and drink

CHAPTER 5

connoisseur
a competent critic or well-equipped judge of a specific subject
smuggler
a person who moves goods or animals out of a country illegally
species
a class of plants or animals with common characteristics
tofu
bean curd

zygodactylous

having two forward and two backward pointing toes

CHAPTER 6

crown

the topmost part of a parrot's head

Elvis

The King of Rock and Roll

junk

a Chinese sailing boat with high stern and shallow draft

pompadour

a style of rolling the hair upward from the forehead

Singapore

an island nation near Malaysia

Tanimbar

an island near Papua New Guinea

CHAPTER 7

astute

shrewd

aviculturist

a person who raises birds

habitat

the natural element or abode of a plant or animal

mandible

the upper or lower jaw of a bird

Manu National Park

a park in Peru where wild parrots can be observed

poacher

a person who steals animals

prolific

highly productive

sashimi

raw fish, a Japanese delicacy

CHAPTER 8

canopy

the middle layer in a forest

CHAPTER 9

acre

4,840 square yards of land

conservation

official protection of natural resources

corrupt

dishonest, accepting bribes

ethics

pertaining to morality or manner

exploit

to use unfairly or unscrupulously to further one's own profit or interest

gazelle

a small, graceful, soft-eyed antelope

instinct

a natural or inborn urge or motivation

organic

of natural composition

predator

an animal that preys on another animal

pupa

the second stage of an insect's development from larva to adult form

steelhead

an ocean-going rainbow trout

succinct

concise, condensed

wildebeest

a gnu; an African oxlike antelope

CHAPTER 10

aviary

a building for the keeping of birds

consciousness

state of being awake and aware

cucaracha

Spanish for cockroach

domestic

a parrot raised in an aviary for the pet trade

exotic

foreign or strange

incubator

an environment suitable to the hatching of eggs

moi

French for "me"

retail

the price a consumer pays for commodities

ring-tailed cat

a nocturnal predator with a raccoon-like tail

unconditional

absolute, unlimited, unequivocal

vibe

the feeling one projects to others

CHAPTER 11

jaguar

large carnivorous member of the wild cat family

turbulence

disturbed, agitated, in violent commotion

CHAPTER 12

AIDS

a fatal disease that attacks the immune system in human beings

leukemia

cancer of the blood

medicinal

having curative or healing properties

peccary

a wild South American hog

raze

to reduce to the ground, tear down

POSTSCRIPT

medium

one of the means, or channels of communication

GET INVOLVED

A FEW ORGANIZATIONS

If you want to learn more about parrots, or want to become involved with saving the earth's natural resources, here are a few organizations you might contact to help get you started.

PARROT ORGANIZATIONS

American Federation of Aviculture
P.O. Box 56218
Phoenix, AZ 85079-6218
Telephone: (800) 247-3225

Avicultural Society of America
P.O. Box 5516
Riverside, CA 92517-5516
Telephone: (909) 780-4102

Canadian World Parrot Trust
P. O. Box 29
Mount Hope,
Ontario
Canada LOR 1WO
E-MAIL: cwparrot@wchat.on.ca

International Aviculturists Society
P. O. Box 280383
Memphis, TN 38168
Telephone: (901) 872-7612

National Audubon Society
700 Broadway
New York, NY 10003
Telephone: (212) 979-3000

World Bird Sanctuary
P.O. Box 270270
St. Louis, MO 63127
Telephone: (314) 938-6193

World Parrot Trust UK
Glanmor House
Hayle, Cornwall TR27 4HY
England
Telephone: 01144 1-0736-753365

World Parrot Trust USA
P. O. Box 341141
Memphis, TN 38184
Telephone/FAX: (901) 873-3616
E-MAIL: cwebb@wsp1.wspice.com

ENVIRONMENTAL ORGANIZATIONS

Ancient Forest International
P.O. Box 1850
Redway, CA 95560
Telephone: (707) 923-3015

Conservation International
1015 18th St. NW, Suite 1000
Washington, DC 20036
Telephone: (800) 406-2306

Defenders of Wildlife
1101 14th Street, NW, #1400
Washington, DC 20005
Telephone: (202) 789-2844

Earth Island Institute
300 Broadway, Suite 28
San Francisco, CA 94133-3312
Telephone: (415) 788-3666

Environmental Defense Fund
257 Park Ave. South
New York, NY 10010
Telephone: (212) 505-2100

Greenpeace USA
1436 U Street NW
Washington, DC 20009
Telephone: (202) 462-1177

International Primate Protection League
P.O. Box 766
Summerville, SC 29484
Telephone: (803) 871-2280

National Wildlife Federation
1400 Sixteenth Street NW
Washington, DC 20036
Telephone: (800) 588-1650,
(202) 797-6800

The Nature Conservancy
1815 North Lynn Street
Arlington, VA 22209
Telephone: (703) 841-5300

Rainforest Action Network
450 Sansome Street, Suite 700
San Francisco, CA 94111
Telephone: (415) 398-4404

The Sierra Club
730 Polk St.
San Francisco, CA 94109
Telephone: (415) 776-2211

World Wildlife Fund
1250 24th St., NW
Washington, DC 20037
Telephone: (202)293-4800

WHAT ARE THOSE PARTS CALLED?

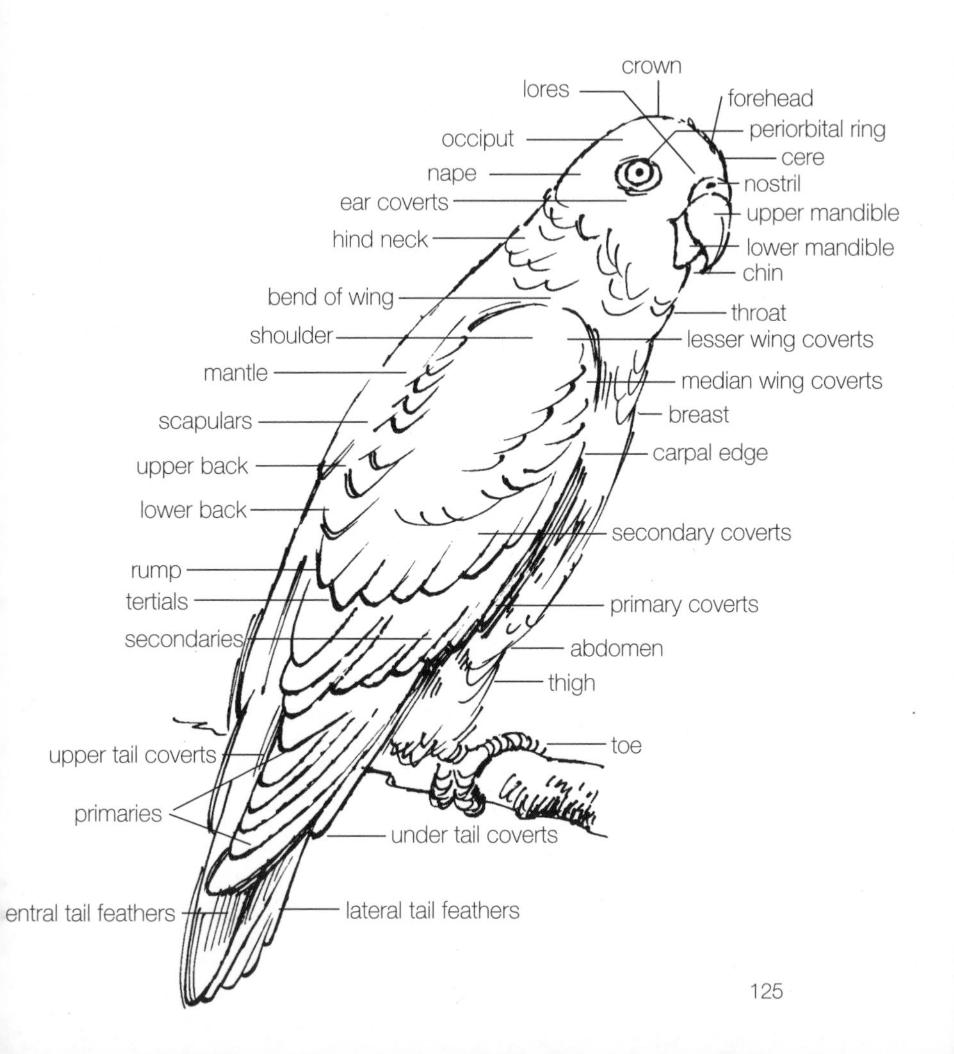

Order form

FAX orders: (916) 478-1360

Telephone orders: (916) 478-1450

On-line orders: deercrk@nccn.net

Postal orders:

Deer Creek Publishing
PO Box 2402
Nevada City, CA 95959

Please send ______ copies of *What the Parrot Told Alice* @ $11.95 each to me at the following address:

Name ____________________

Address ____________________

City ______ State ______ Zip ______ – ______

Please send ______ gift copies of *What the Parrot Told Alice* @ $11.95 each to:

Name ____________________

Address ____________________

City ______ State ______ Zip ______ – ______

Enclose gift card signed as follows:

____

____

Sales tax

Please add 7.25% (.87¢ ea.) for books shipped to California.

Shipping

Book rate: $2.00 for first book and 75 cents for each additional book to same address. Surface shipping may take three to four weeks. Priority mail: $3.50 per book.

Payment

_____ check (make check payable to Deer Creek Publishing)

_____ credit card (circle one) VISA MasterCard

Card number: ____________________

Name on card: ____________________ Exp. date: _____/______

Siignature: ____________________